I0665179

EVERYONE'S OUT TO GET YOU WHEN YOU'RE

STAYING ON TOP

A VALERIEL INVESTIGATIONS NOVEL

ELIZABETH CORRIGAN

Staying on Top
Copyright © 2018 by Elizabeth Corrigan. All rights reserved.
First Print Edition: September 2018

ISBN: 978-0-9862573-5-3

Cover and Formatting: Streetlight Graphics

No part of this book may be reproduced, scanned, or distributed in any printed or electronic form without permission. Please do not participate in or encourage piracy of copyrighted materials in violation of the author's rights. Thank you for respecting the hard work of this author.

This is a work of fiction. Names, characters, places, and incidents either are the product of the author's imagination or are used fictitiously, and any resemblance to locales, events, business establishments, or actual persons—living or dead—is entirely coincidental.

PROLOGUE

BEATRIN ORIOLE *NEE* DEVALERIEL STOOD in the lavish bathroom attached to her childhood bedroom and splashed water on her face. She stared at her severe pixie cut and heavily mascaraed hazel eyes and tried not to notice how her reflection in the gilt-framed mirror looked so much older than it used to. She remembered the young girl with her long, curled brown hair and smooth, rosy skin, who could never imagine getting crow's feet around her eyes. If she'd thought about it, Beatrin DeValeriel would have said she might someday get laugh lines.

No one would suggest that Beatrin Oriole had laugh lines.

At least I look better than I did on my wedding day. She touched up the foundation around her eyes. *Wrinkles are one thing, but no one looks good in tears.*

Somehow, she could never come up to this room without thinking of her wedding day, which should have been reason enough to avoid it. Yet this suite of rooms was the only place left in the world that felt like it belonged to her. It was in her brother's estate, of course, but Baurus would never change it or keep her away from it if she really wanted it, so she found herself seeking its familiarity whenever Baurus decided to hold a gala, which was all too frequently these days.

I thought after Callista died... Well, I don't know what I thought.

Beatrin had expected the queen's death would affect her brother. After all, he had been her most frequent and infamous lover, if not her only one, and he adored her, despite her infinite flaws. If he had holed himself up in his estate or gone on an extended vacation overseas or even become a public drunkard, she would have understood.

Instead, he had decided that if he couldn't shock society by sleeping with his cousin's wife, he was going to find as many other ways to do it as he could. He'd started attending Assembly meetings, and at first, Beatrin had thought he was finally taking his hereditary duty seriously. But then he started siding with the Merchants as often as he did with the Imperials, and an equal share of the time, he started going off about creating laws to help the commoners instead of exclusively the wealthy. Beatrin had hoped his brief stint of civic-mindedness would pass, but six months after his stint in a Valeriel holding cell, he seemed determined to stay the course.

At least he doesn't expect people to go along with his insanity.

All of this would have been embarrassing enough if Baurus had at least made an effort to keep out of the *Valeriel Tribune*, but he'd begun throwing an endless stream of galas, all of which made the front page of the Society section. Beatrin had hoped that part of his motivation was seeking a wife to soften his image, but despite all the press, his name hadn't been linked with any woman's for more than an idle moment of speculation.

Of course, it wasn't the galas that were the problem so much as the people he invited. At first, he asked a few of his new Merchant cronies from the Assembly. Beatrin had managed to grit her teeth through these. Zevier Marsh and Travor Skid might have worked in trades, but they were part of the government, and they knew their place. Baurus had crossed a line tonight, though, when he invited Entertainers.

No, she thought. *I will not even acknowledge that with a capital letter. This new generation making money off moving pictures and rock bands and whatever else may be trying to form their own guild to rival the Merchants and the Imperials, but I will never acknowledge them.*

Beatrin didn't know how Baurus had met Coelis Crest, Philindra Dixie, and Mandrick Pane, but Baurus had put them on the guest list for his autumnal equinox gala. *And of course, the fools didn't have the decency to realize they weren't supposed to come—not that Baurus helped matters by treating them like treasured friends.*

In her heart of hearts, Beatrin knew that part of the reason she resented the entertainers so much was that she envied them. They were the young and beautiful up-and-comers, with wealth that didn't come with years of Imperial traditions and obligations. She wondered if Baurus felt as old as she did, standing next to this new generation, but she knew he didn't. He was a man and considered the most eligible bachelor in the city, even though he was thirty-five. She, on the other hand, would be forty in another two months, and five minutes of dabbing had not covered the crow's feet at the corners of her eyes.

She almost wished her mother were there because the Dowager Duchess Augustille DeValeriel was the only person who despaired of Baurus as much as Beatrin did. Baurus didn't listen to either one of them, but sometimes, Beatrin appreciated having someone sympathize with her.

Of course, I'm not so much someone Mother commiserates with as complains at—not that I can blame her. I, unlike Baurus, listen to her. Somehow, though, that meant that Beatrin got blamed for Baurus's flaws as well as her own, even though she had been a perfect Imperial and daughter in the twenty years since her forcible removal from the company of Garson Grey.

Beatrin stifled something she wasn't sure was a laugh or a cry. *That's the kicker, of course: that Garson is here to witness my humiliation.* The *Valeriel Tribune*'s premier reporter on the social life of the city's elite, and Beatrin's former lover, attended most high-society parties, and never had she seen him fawn over anyone like he did over Coelis Crest.

After that, Beatrin had consumed a few more drinks than was appropriate for someone of her station and decided to come up here to avoid embarrassing herself. And so she had come full circle because between the memory of the party and the crow's feet in the mirror, she wanted another drink.

Besides, I need to get back to the party before anyone notices my absence.

She couldn't help taking a minute to gaze about her old bedroom. It looked as austere as the day she'd left, all mauve and mahogany, as her mother had decided befitted the daughter of a prince. None of the Imperial houses of Valeriel used pink as a color, but the DeValeriel black and red was reserved for the men of the line.

The only thing out of place was the slightly ajar closet door. She could have let it be, but somehow, it seemed the one thing that evening she could control. She moved toward the door and pushed it shut. When the latch didn't click as she expected, she pushed again, harder this time.

The door bounced back, and something fell out. *That's odd. That looks like a hand. If one of those idiots got drunk and came up to my room and... shut themselves in the closet?* Even as she thought the words, she realized how little sense they made. She pulled open the door.

A body tumbled out.

Beatrin took in the blond hair, the garish pink dress

that clashed horribly with the room's tasteful mauve, and the ashen skin too pale to exist on a living person.

Fabulous. Starlet Coelis Crest had not only had the audacity to come to a gala she had no business attending, but while she was there, she had the poor taste to get murdered.

CHAPTER 1

"WELL, I GUESS THIS IS good night."

Kadin Stone stood on the front stoop of her brother's townhouse and reminded herself that she *wanted* her date to kiss her.

The night was balmy despite the calendar switching to autumn earlier that day. A moon hung nearly full in the west while the one in the east showed barely a sliver. Stars twinkled between them in the darkening blue sky of late evening. All in all, the night was perfect, yet Kadin couldn't wait for it to be over.

This is not how you're supposed to feel, she told herself. *You should be happy you've held onto a boyfriend for six months. If things continue, he'll propose in the next few months.*

Somehow, no matter how many times she gave herself this lecture, her stomach did a swan dive every time she thought of spending the rest of her life married to Dahran White. She didn't object to marriage in general, she told herself, and she was too practical to expect the butterflies-in-her-stomach kind of romance her friend Trinithy Gold imagined with every gentleman who took her out.

I just want someone who doesn't condescend to the waitstaff. Kadin ground her teeth at the memory of Dahran chewing out their waitress that evening for splashing a drop of water on the table. *Is that too much to ask?*

"I suppose it must be." Dahran's voice held disappointment, and Kadin felt a stab of guilt. She should be as happy to spend time with him as he was to spend time with her.

Not that I understand why he likes me so much. I'm not exactly a scintillating conversationalist on these dates. Mostly, he did the talking, while she did the looking pretty. She guessed that was all he wanted in a girlfriend, which at least meant the hours she spent primping for their dates wasn't in vain. Her red hair did not curl itself. Her pale skin did not blush delicately on its own, and the lashes around her brown eyes did not curl so prettily without mascara.

Kadin took a step back toward the door. "I had a great time. We'll have to do it again some time." She laughed to show she was kidding. They had plans to try out a new club the next evening and to go to the autocar race on Saturday, in addition to seeing each other every day at work.

"Come here." Dahran barely spoke the words as warning before he pulled her closer, but they were enough that she avoided tensing in his arms.

Standing so close to him, she wondered if he put nearly as much effort into his appearance as she did. She suspected he didn't and added it to the list of things she would try not to resent him for. His slicked-down dark-brown hair and crystal-blue eyes had most of the girls in the office swooning, and the straight white teeth of his killer smile had more than one of the sideways men turning their eyes his way as well.

Dahran's lips descended on hers, and she did her best to make her mouth warm and inviting, as if she had any idea how to do that. His arms went around her, and she'd focused her defenses so much on not stiffening that she almost jumped in surprise when he slid his tongue into her mouth. She jerked her jaw fast enough that she didn't clamp her incisors down on the offending organ, but her normal teeth squeaked against his perfect ones, which she suspected was not the least bit sexy. He must not have been too offended, though, because he maintained the kiss for a few moments longer, and when it ended, he let out a sigh.

"Kay, you're amazing," Dahran whispered against her forehead.

Am I? She didn't feel particularly amazing. She felt phony. She felt passive. She felt like Dahran was an idiot for not realizing that she could barely stand to have him touch her.

As she did when she started having uncharitable thoughts about Dahran, Kadin remembered Trinithy's list of his virtues. *He's handsome. He's employed. We have work interests in common. He likes me. And I'm not as pretty as Trinithy, so I can't just dump every guy who shows an interest in me.*

Dahran reached into his coat. "I wasn't going to do this now. I was going to wait for the perfect moment, but every moment with you is perfect."

Holy shit! Kadin chastised herself for swearing. *He's going to propose* right now. Dahran continued to blather, but her heartbeat was so loud and her breathing so shallow that she couldn't listen to what he was saying

Oh, Deity save me. I can't marry him. I can't.

You have to, you idiot. Have you been leading him on all this time? You need to get married. You need to move out of your brother's house. What are you waiting for, anyway— Duke Baurus himself to come down off his Imperial Estate and sweep you away from your life? If he planned to do it, he would have done it six months ago.

She didn't know where that thought came from. After her brief interaction with Duke Baurus in the wake of his lover's murder, she might have harbored a fantasy or two about him. After all, she'd believed he hadn't murdered Queen Callista when no one else had. But she knew she was merely a helpful commoner to him. Dahran was reality, and if he was asking her to marry him, she had to say yes.

Time seemed to slow. Kadin felt every drop of saliva trickle down her throat as her mouth went dry. Dahran's arm slid out of his coat as he ever so carefully bent his knee.

The door behind Kadin opened with a creak and a whoosh, and with this surprise, she did jump.

"Kadin Stone! Thank the Deity you're home! What is Duke Baurus DeValeriel doing in my living room?"

With Octavira's arrival, the rest of the world resumed its normal speed. Kadin couldn't fathom her sister-in-law ever moving in slow motion. Dahran's hand emerged empty from his coat, and he used it to cover his mouth as he cleared his throat. The screen door swung closed behind Octavira with a swish and a slam. Kadin, however, felt that the time it took her to turn around and face Octavira lasted longer than any sleepless night.

Oh, of course, she thought as she took in first the red rose pattern on Octavira's full white skirt, then the red-nailed hands on Octavira's hips, and finally the horrified "Os" of Octavira's painted red lips and kohl-lined eyes beneath her dark brown updo. *I'm dreaming.*

She had to be dreaming. In the real world, Dahran White's proposal would not be interrupted by the duke of the city appearing in her life after six months' absence.

But the pounding of her heart and the thin layer of moisture on her palms felt more real than anything that occurred in a dream. She remembered everything that happened that day and knew how she had gotten there. Her teeth weren't falling out, she couldn't fly, and she had that solid, real-life feeling that dream-Kadin could never quite muster.

And it is *just like Baurus to show up in the nick of time to rescue me, like a prince out of a fairy tale or at least someone whose life is so privileged he wouldn't dare show up at any time except the exact right one.*

"I... I don't know?" said Kadin when she finally found her voice, or at least half of it. "You should ask him."

"I did." Octavira's hiss indicated she feared the duke overhearing.

Fair. The living room is right on the other side of that drafty door.

"He said he was here to see you," said Octavira.

"Oh." Kadin's head felt floaty, as if maybe she were in a dream after all. "Then I guess he's here to see me." Her heart pounded for what felt like the fiftieth time that evening, except this time excitement, rather than terror, drove its motions. One of the most important men in the city wanted to see her.

You don't care how important he is, a traitorous voice inside her whispered. *You're excited that* Baurus *wants to see you.*

"Yes, but what does he want?" Octavira managed to emphasize the "s" in the word "want," which Kadin found impressive.

"I... don't know." Kadin said again, and her voice had returned to its full timbre. "I guess I'd better go find out."

Kadin brushed past Octavira and pulled open the screen door then pushed open the heavier wooden door behind it. She had almost forgotten Dahran's and Octavira's presences when Octavira said, "Yes, I think we've kept His Grace waiting long enough."

Kadin stepped into the homey living room, appreciating the slight increase in temperature from the outside. The scent of the apple pie Octavira must have made for dinner still hung in the air. Kadin barely took in the usual sights and smells of home, though, so focused was she on the red-and-black-clad figure standing in the middle of the room.

The society glossies wrote page after page about how handsome Baurus DeValeriel was, but Kadin, for her part, didn't see it. She had known much more classically attractive men—Dahran White, for example. What Baurus had—and what Kadin found so much more appealing than mere handsomeness—was energy, a palpable force that radiated from every pore of his body. It electrified the room around him and made people forget that his nose was a little too big, his hazel eyes a little too far apart, and his jaw a little too square.

"No, I won't sit, my good woman. I—" Baurus's features animated when he saw that it was not Octavira who had entered the room. "Kadin!" He didn't smile, but Kadin nonetheless got the impression he was pleased to see her.

"Indeed, Your Grace." Kadin picked up the hesitation in her voice. What was the proper address for a duke who stormed in and out of her life as he wanted? She wondered if she should curtsy. She had no doubt Trinithy or Octavira could have pulled off beautiful curtsies, owing to the full skirts they wore. Since tapered skirts made Kadin's sturdy legs look less like tree trunks, she opted to wear them, but they made curtsying difficult.

The duke's brow creased. "I told you to stop calling me that. You saved me from a life sentence for a murder I didn't commit, remember? We don't stand on ceremony."

"I... of course, your—Baurus." Kadin hadn't realized they stood on anything anymore, but she wasn't going to contradict him.

"You're upset that I didn't call, aren't you?" Baurus ran his fingers through his hair, dislodging the perfectly slicked-down curls. "That always happens in those silly novels Bay and her friends read. Men don't call, and women get all upset about it. But I said to myself, 'Kadin's not like that. She'll understand I have to lay some groundwork first.' Tell me you understand."

She didn't understand, at least, not what he was babbling about. She had never expected him to call her. He was a duke, for pity's sake. She didn't imagine he even talked on a phone so much as had people do it for him.

"Of course."

Baurus nodded. Apparently, it was Kadin's night for bluffing men. He didn't calm, though. Kadin didn't think he ever calmed.

"I wanted to invite you tonight, but I need to work up to that. I invited some actors, and of course, that's the problem."

Kadin could barely follow what he was saying, which wasn't surprising. Given Baurus's flushed face and animated hands, she suspected he didn't know what he was saying, either.

"Some actors are the problem?" asked Kadin. "Didn't you invite them?"

The duke's social recognition of the Entertainers Guild had filled the tabloids for the past week, and Kadin hated that she knew that. Six months ago, her friend Olivan King's constant gossiping about Imperials had gone in one ear and out the other, but these days, her memory proved sticky where Baurus DeValeriel was concerned.

"Yes!" Baurus threw his hands in the air. "I didn't realize one of them was going to turn up dead!"

"I don't... Wait, what?" Kadin held an image of Imperial galas as stately affairs that, no doubt, bore little resemblance to reality. The ultra-rich probably engaged in all kinds of scandalous—and dangerous—behavior. "What kind of party was this?

Baurus held up his hands in defense. "Not the kind of party where someone dies! Beatrin wouldn't have it. She thinks I live to make her life miserable, but I make people take the hard drug use elsewhere. No, no, no. The actress got murdered. What was her name again? Something Crest? Shelly? No, Coelis. Coelis Crest."

Kadin's mouth dropped open. "You left a party you hosted after it had turned into a crime scene? You can't do that! You're a material witness!"

Baurus snapped his fingers and pointed at her. "See, that's why I did. I need you. I don't know anything about solving murders. I need the most brilliant investigative mind in the city on this, and near as I can tell, that's you."

"I am not the most brilliant investigative mind in the city! I'm a detective's aide. I follow my boss around, take notes"—*and solve half his cases*—"and bring him his java."

Baurus waved a hand. "You're the only detective I know personally who has ever solved a murder, and I saw a whole bunch who didn't back during that whole Callista affair. And these idiots from CrimeSolve look like they're cut from the same cloth—a bunch of suits more interested in getting their names in the paper than actually solving crimes. I need you."

Kadin didn't know where to start. Since when did Baurus dismiss the death of the love of his life as "that whole Callista affair"? And what did he mean, he needed her? He needed a detective to solve the murder, but it didn't have to be her. *He said that last word with such intensity, though.*

"Wait, you hired CrimeSolve already, and you're still trying to hire me? Why do you need two detective agencies?"

"I don't. I only planned to hire you, but Bay found the body, and she called CrimeSolve before she even talked to me. I argued with her about it, but she was in a mood before she found the body."

Kadin almost opened her next sentence with his name, but she couldn't quite bring herself to say it with the called-for tone of exasperation. "CrimeSolve is the biggest, most well-regarded detective agency in the kingdom. They are perfectly capable of handling this without me!"

Wait, why am I arguing against this? It's a murder. Solving murders is my job.

You're arguing because you don't want Baurus DeValeriel to waltz back into your life and then waltz right back out again, that's why. It's better if he just goes now.

"If I might interject..."

The interruption came from the kitchen doorway. Dahran stood there, looking rather like a child in a candy store. *Octavira must have let him in the back way.*

Dahran moved into the room and put his arm around Kadin. "Detective agencies often work together on cases if there are competing interests involved, as it sounds like there may be in your case, Your Grace. Kay here may not realize that because she's only an aide—and a rather new one at that." *Women, what can you do?* said Dahran's look.

Baurus's jaw clenched, and Kadin suspected she was not the only one who wanted to smack that smug look off Dahran's face.

Handsome. Employed. Things in common. Likes you.

"I, however, am a full detective," Dahran continued. "And I would be happy to take on the role of lead detective for this case."

Dahran held out the hand that was not wound around Kadin to the duke.

Baurus kept his gaze on Kadin. "So you'll come?"

"I'll come. I just need to make one call first."

CHAPTER 2

"**Q**UICK, TELL ME EVERYTHING YOU know about Coelis Crest!" Kadin said into the telephone.

"Do you have any idea what time it is?" asked the voice on the other end of the line. "I need my beauty sleep, you know."

Kadin glanced at the rooster-shaped clock above the kitchen sink.

"The day you're getting your beauty sleep this early on a Saturday night is the day I sprout wings and join the devil's entourage. I'm surprised you're even home."

Kadin could practically hear Olivan King stretching out on his red leather sofa. "Well, ordinarily I would be out, but tonight Vinnie came over, and we—"

"Too much information. Back to the subject at hand." The last thing Kadin wanted to discuss with Olivan, even when she wasn't in a hurry, was his boyfriend.

This time she heard the squeak of the sofa as Olivan sat up. "I wasn't going to say anything dirty! Honestly, Kay, I don't know what your problem with Vinnie is. Sometimes I swear he likes you better than he likes me."

Kadin doubted that was true, but she did share a closeness with Vinnie that Olivan did not. She knew Vinnie's deepest secret: there was no such person as Vinnie Royal, and there never had been. He was the Merchant alter ego of King Ralvin DeValeriel, a man who spent all his public time wearing formal robes and face makeup so that no one would realize he spent his days parading around as a sideways man who owned part of the newspaper.

Kadin did like Ralvin. She understood that he could never be his true self in a nation that expected its monarch to sire an heir. In the six months since she'd learned his secret, he had become one of her best friends. She hated that he was dating one of her friends, though, both because she hated lying to Olivan and because the relationship would never work out long term. So Kadin did what she could, which was largely ignore the issue.

"I don't have a problem with Vinnie." *Lie, lie, lie.* "But I'm in a bit of a hurry. Can you tell me everything you know about Coelis Crest?"

"Really, Kay? An entertainer? You know I have better taste than that." Despite the fact that he was dating someone he thought was a Merchant, Olivan was a perennial supporter of the Imperials and general believer in their superiority over mere commoners, himself included.

"I know that you read any gossip glossy you can get your hands on, no matter who it's about." Kadin thought of Olivan's filing cabinets at work, which, instead of containing personnel data, were filled with painstakingly organized articles on every famous person in the city. "It's a matter of pride."

"Fine, fine. You know I keep my best stuff at the office, but I've got a few things here I haven't had time to catalogue yet." From Olivan's end came the sound of rustling papers, as he no doubt rummaged through some of the glossies he always had at his fingertips. "Hey, if you need sudden information about Coelis, does this mean she's involved in a murder? Victim or perp? Or just a person of interest? Ooh, ooh! Does she have a stalker?"

"Ollie, you know I can't reveal the details of a case."

"So there *is* a case!" Kadin heard the fiendish smile in Olivan's voice. "Face it. I know now, and if you don't tell me, I will start spreading the most outrageous rumors I can think of."

Kadin knew Olivan didn't mean that as a threat so much as a warning. He had a social network that rivaled society columnist Garson Grey's and was incapable of discretion. He'd make up some hypothetical, forget to throw in enough "maybes," and a rumor would be born.

Kadin wasn't concerned about the damage to Coelis Crest's reputation—she was dead, so she probably didn't care—but Kadin worried that any stories that got out about Coelis might waste valuable detective hours. Kadin had learned over the past six months that trails went cold quickly during a murder investigation.

"Okay, fine. I'll tell you, but you have to *swear* not to breathe a word of this to anyone."

Kadin imagined Olivan drawing an "X" over his chest with his finger. "I am the soul of discretion."

Kadin turned her gaze up to the ceiling and shook her head. "Yeah, that describes you perfectly."

"You know, you never used to be this sarcastic before you got all famous solving homicides—Holy crap! Was Coelis Crest murdered?"

"I'm not famous. I didn't even get credit for the one big case I solved." In the interests of not wasting time in a murder investigation, Kadin continued before Olivan could argue. "And yes, Coelis Crest was murdered. She was at Baurus DeValeriel's party tonight—"

"I know that. Everyone knows that. Even you know that." Olivan's voice raised in pitch with every word. "How was she murdered? Who did it? Was it grisly? Deity, I can't wait to tell Trinithy. She was saying no good could come of Entertainers at an Imperial gala, but I said—"

"Soul of discretion, remember?" Kadin knew Olivan keeping this news quiet was about as likely as Baurus showing up in her living room, and she was all out of miracles for one evening. *Well, the news will be in all the papers tomorrow, anyway.* Baurus's parties were the talk of the Society pages, and a murder at one was guaranteed front-page news of the *Valeriel Tribune*. "Can you just tell me what you know about Coelis?"

"Coelis Crest, rising film star, considered by many to be the most beautiful woman in the world now that Queen Callista bit the big one." Papers rustled. "Huh. You don't think someone's going after blond bombshells, do you? Because that would be—"

"Ollie. Focus." Kadin didn't want to think the queen's murderer, Herrick Strand, could have committed this murder. *Though he could have... He is still at large.*

"Right. Relevant to your murdery interests, Coelis has two best friends: Philindra Dixie and Mandrick Pane. Both of them were also invited to the duke's party tonight, and the three of them are the only Entertainers to ever get such an invite. So if you want my money on the murderer, it's one of them unless you think an Imperial would kill Coelis for having the audacity to show up at one of their parties."

"That would probably be a bit extreme, even for an Imperial," said Kadin, "though we can't rule out any possibilities at this point."

"Of course not. It's a murder investigation. I've had the training. I know how it goes." Olivan had taken the detective's aide course alongside Kadin, but he had neglected to apply for any aide positions. He said that working in personnel gave him the opportunity to meet more people, which Kadin knew meant it gave him the opportunity to learn more people's secrets. "Anyway, the rumor mill says that Mandrick was sleeping with Coelis because as you know, Entertainers become famous, and no one cares if they stay virgins."

Kadin gasped. "Really? But that's illegal!"

"Apparently there's a black market of doctors who falsify their patients' birth control tests." Kadin could almost see Olivan's offhand shrug. "But you have to make a lot of money to afford a doctor like that, and you never know when he's going to turn on you. You remember the Edeline Arrow incident from last year, of course."

"Not really, no."

"Honestly, Kay. We have got to get you a subscription to at least one glossy. Edeline was an up-and-coming film star. You remember her. Brown hair, dazzling smile?"

"Vaguely."

"Well, she was sleeping with her doctor, and then he found out she was spreading her favors to other men as well, and he outed her about the pills. Now she's Class-D and unemployable. She was on the line for a big film contract too and had to give back the money."

"Okay." Kadin took a moment to think and heard a murmur of conversation from the living room. She remembered that she had left Baurus, Octavira, and Dahran alone in there and decided she should probably wrap this up. "What does this have to do with Coelis Crest?"

"Nothing, directly, except she probably had a doctor like that too, especially if she was sleeping with Mandrick. A lead to follow."

Kadin made a note on the pad on the counter next to the telephone. "Good point. Hey, did you say Vinnie was there? Can I talk to him?"

Olivan stopped breathing for a second, then his air came out in a rush. "You're on a rush-rush murder investigation, and you want to take time to talk to my boyfriend? Whom you don't even like?"

"I never said I didn't like him. I just think you and he are wrong for each other. That's all. Can you put him on?"

Olivan huffed. "Fine, but one of these days, you're going to tell me why you're so against me having a rich and handsome man in my life." Olivan's next words were muffled, as if he were covering the phone as he called into the next room. "Vinnie? Kadin wants to talk to you!" After an even more muffled statement that Kadin couldn't make out, Olivan said, "How should I know? Ask her!"

"Hello?" A strong voice, pitched slightly higher than his cousin's, sounded on the other end of the phone. "Kadin?"

Kadin took a deep breath. "Hey, I figured since you were there, I'd let you know that your cousin showed up at my house tonight."

"Oh?"

Ralvin's one syllable conveyed a sentence: "I am very interested in what you are saying but feigning much less interest because my boyfriend, who has no idea why you want to talk to me, is still in the room."

Kadin hadn't known how Ralvin would react. Six months after its inception, she was still navigating her relationship with the king. This was the second time his two alter egos' paths had crossed in her life, the first being the incident that had led her to discover his dual identity in the first place. Theoretically, Ralvin should have been able to know Kadin and still live his two separate lives. He was royalty, and she was as common as common came.

"Apparently, Coelis Crest died at his party tonight, and he's calling me—well, Valeriel Investigations—in to investigate."

"Hm."

Translation: "That's very bad, and it's extra bad that he's bothering you about this. I'd like to say more, but boyfriend still in the room."

"I have to go. I need to call Jace—you remember our forensic analyst? —because that's what I told Baurus and Dahran I was doing in the first place. Anyway, I figured you'd want to know before you heard about it in the papers or before Ollie opens his big mouth, which I'm sure he's going to do as soon as you get off the phone."

"Probably." Ralvin's voice held a smile.

"Look, call me tomorrow, if you can get away and want to talk more about this."

"Will do." His breathing disappeared from the other end of the line as he handed the phone back to Olivan.

"What was that all about?" asked Olivan.

"I just wanted to tell him something." Kadin sounded defensive, even to her own ears. "It's not that big a deal."

"You're in the middle of a murder investigation, and you want to talk to Vinnie, who knows nothing about murder. What, did you want him to keep it out of the *Tribune*? You know he doesn't have that much control over what goes in it." Olivan's voice had taken on a biting tone, and Kadin decided she had to get off the phone with him. If Ralvin wanted to date Olivan, that meant dealing with him when he was in one of his sarcastic moods.

She said the one thing she could think of to mollify her friend. "I have to go now, but I promise to call you tomorrow and tell you everything."

"You'd better." Olivan hung up.

Kadin also hung up, though she immediately picked up the phone again, this time dialing Jace Combs's number.

"Do you have any idea what time it is?"

Kadin didn't even need to glance at the rooster to know this time. "Yes, I do. But when Baurus DeValeriel shows up in your living room, demanding you solve a murder for him, you do it."

CHAPTER 3

KADIN HAD WORRIED THAT BAURUS and Dahran would argue about who drove her over to the DeValeriel estate, but to Kadin's relief, Dahran wanted to ride in Baurus's convertible, even if he did have to sit in the back.

"Ladies up front," Baurus had said, though Kadin suspected he wanted to get Dahran's goat more than demonstrate chivalry.

"This is ridiculous," Dahran said for the fifth or sixth time as Baurus turned into the Imperial District. "My legs are longer than hers. I shouldn't be cramped back here."

Kadin wanted to be enjoying the trip in the luxurious vehicle she suspected cost more than her annual salary. The seats were the softest leather she'd ever encountered, and the drop top allowed for a lovely view of the starry night. Instead, she felt her cheeks flush redder every time Dahran complained. She wondered what Baurus thought but wasn't brave enough to look at him to find out.

Eventually, they turned into the long drive leading up to the DeValeriel estate. As Kadin took in the grand residence with its marble columns and red-and-black heraldry, she realized she hadn't been to Baurus's home before. The view gave her a thrill she didn't quite understand, and since their arrival meant an end to Dahran's whining, she had never been so glad to see a place in her life—at least until she saw the yellow car parked on the curb. *I guess CrimeSolve beat us here.*

Baurus pulled the convertible up behind the CrimeSolve car and hopped out. Kadin hurried to follow suit.

"You're double-parked!" she said.

"Eh, the valet will take care of it." Baurus flashed her a grin. "Besides, it's not like anyone can leave. This is a murder investigation."

You left, thought Kadin, but she was well aware that the rules that applied to normal people didn't apply to Baurus DeValeriel.

Baurus bounded up the stairs of his manor, and Kadin looked back to make sure Dahran had extricated himself from the back seat before turning to follow. As soon as Baurus reached the door, someone on the other side opened it. Kadin recognized the man as Baurus's butler from the duke's house in the Merchant district.

"Your Grace has returned." The butler gave a small bow and a reproachful look. "Things are rather chaotic here."

Baurus's grin widened. "That's why I brought the best homicide detective in Valeriel back with me."

"Why, thank you," said Dahran.

Baurus didn't spare Dahran a glance. "I didn't mean you. Oh, hey," he said to his butler. "If you see a surly-looking pretty boy with a medical kit, let him in as well."

Kadin stepped into the grand hall after Baurus, unsurprised to see a plethora of people in formal wear. She tried not to stare overmuch at the gowns, but she could tell that the finest dress in her closet could not hold a candle to these shimmering, one-of-a-kind creations. Baurus zeroed in on a pretty woman with light-brown hair and wearing a sequined purple dress, whom Kadin recognized as Lady Elyesse Imbolc.

"Where's Bay?" asked Baurus.

Lady Elyesse cringed. Even scrunched up, her delicate

features remained beautiful. "By the bar. She's not taking any of this well."

A buzz of conversation surrounded Kadin as she followed Baurus to wherever the bar was. She told herself that these people were not talking about her. They had witnessed a murder and had better things to worry about than a commoner in their midst, but she still felt horribly plain, even in her best date clothes.

Baurus led Kadin and Dahran into a room off the main hall, where a permanent bar was set up. *Baurus must host a lot of galas to dedicate a whole room to a bar. Of course, I knew that. Ollie tells me about all of them. And these days, I even listen.*

The black-and-red-clad bartender handed a clear beverage to a woman in her late thirties with a dark-brown pixie cut, but before she could take it, a man with fiery-red hair whisked it away from her. "I think you've had enough, Bay," he said.

"I don't." Beatrin Oriole snatched the glass back from the man and downed it in one swallow. "I don't know why you care, anyway. Shouldn't you be off collecting horrible rumors to spread all over the city?"

Aha. This must be Garson Grey, society writer extraordinaire. Rumor had him in a relationship with Beatrin Oriole back when she was Beatrin DeValeriel, and from the look on his face, the feelings between them were not entirely in the past.

"Probably, but I hate seeing you like this." Grey glanced back at the doorway. He nodded at Baurus then turned back to Beatrin. "Looks like your brother wants to talk to you."

The duchess looked up, bleary-eyed. Her gaze brushed past Baurus and landed on Kadin. Beatrin turned back to the bar and buried her head in her arms. "Of course, he had to bring her."

Grey glanced from Beatrin to Baurus and back again.

"Well, I think I have some gossip to collect. Murder and all. Very exciting." He gave the top of Beatrin's head a small smile. "Let me know if you need anything, Bay."

The duchess mumbled something that sounded like "Don't call me that."

After Grey left, Beatrin sat back up and wobbled around to face Baurus. "Nice of you to come back, brother."

Baurus scowled. "I told you. I needed to go get Kadin."

"And of course, you couldn't have called like a normal person," Beatrin slurred.

Kadin had her doubts about whether anyone at this gala had the faintest idea what it was like to be a normal person, but from what she could tell, Baurus, at least, thought of himself as ordinary. Dukes who thought themselves above commoners didn't show up in said commoners' living rooms.

"Of course, I called first," said Baurus. "No one answered the phone."

Beatrin gave an exaggerated sigh and had to balance herself against the bar as she listed to the side. "So you went out in person. I called a real detective agency, one that actually answers their phone at all hours for an emergency."

"Valeriel Investigations has a twenty-four-hour—"

Kadin waved at Dahran to be quiet. She had a sinking suspicion that Baurus had not tried to call Valeriel Investigations. He had tried to call *her*, which she found unsettling on a number of levels.

Kadin cleared her throat. "So can we see the body? Interview the witnesses?"

"Absolutely!" said Baurus at the same time that Beatrin said, "No."

"Bay, don't be difficult." Baurus turned to Kadin. "She found the body, so she's understandably somewhat upset."

And drunk, thought Kadin, though she couldn't blame the duchess. Kadin had met any number of people who

29

had found dead bodies in the past six months, and a good proportion of them had been drunk by the time she arrived.

"Lady Beatrin," said Dahran, "if we could ask you a few questions—"

"I'll talk to the real detectives, thank you very much." Beatrin turned back to the bar and beckoned the bartender for another drink.

Baurus shook his head but still appeared chipper. "She's going to regret all that drinking in the morning. She gets the worst hangovers. Come on. I'll take you to where we found the body."

As the three of them left the room, Kadin thought she heard Beatrin mutter, "Where *I* found the body."

They crossed back out into the main hall, where the tension among the nobles had intensified. Lady Elyesse joined them and kept pace with Baurus as he headed toward the black marble staircase.

"When are you going to let everyone leave?" she asked. "The investigators have been here for over an hour. They've gotten everyone's names. Are you really going to keep us on lockdown all night?"

A frown marred Baurus's face. "The investigator I want on this case just got here. People can leave when she says they can go."

Elyesse looked back at Kadin, her mouth curved in a wistful twist. "You're going to be difficult, aren't you?" she said, and Kadin wasn't sure whether Elyesse addressed Kadin or Baurus.

"Don't be silly, Ely." Baurus leaned over and kissed her on the cheek. "I'm never difficult. Keep everyone calm for a bit longer. You're good at that."

Elyesse gave Baurus an indulgent smile and headed back into the crowd. Baurus started up the staircase, and Kadin followed. She marveled that she had gotten better at walking in heels over the last six months. Not that long ago, she would have tripped over her stilettos as they dug into the plush red carpet.

Kadin glanced down the stairs just in time to see the door open and the most handsome man she had ever known walk into the foyer. Jace Combs might have been wearing common clothes—ones that didn't even match, as if he had thrown them on in a hurry when she'd called, which he probably had—but he could never look out of place at a gathering such as this. His soft blond hair and angelic features seemed more out of place at the run-of-the-mill office building.

Too bad that he's married to the world's biggest sub-D and that he's a class-A jerk. She regretted the thought as soon as it came out, especially because it wasn't true. Jace wasn't the cheeriest guy she knew, but he cared about helping people and solving crimes. He didn't have anywhere near Dahran's level of self-centeredness.

Employed. Good-looking. Interests in common. Likes me, Kadin reminded herself as she waved Jace over.

"What's going on?" Jace spoke quietly enough that only Kadin could hear him. "And why are we here if CrimeSolve is?"

Kadin responded in equally hushed tones. "Lady Beatrin called CrimeSolve, and Baurus called us." *Or showed up in my living room, as the case may be.* "We'll just have to collaborate."

Jace snorted. "CrimeSolve doesn't collaborate, but that's fine with me. I like to stay out of these high-profile murder cases."

Kadin glanced up the stairs. Baurus had reached the top and was turning left. "I don't think we have a lot of choice. Baurus wants us on this case, and what Baurus wants, Baurus gets."

"We'll see," said Jace as he and Kadin rounded the corner after Baurus and Dahran. "For my part, I'm going to take whatever samples I can now because I doubt I'll be seeing that body again after tonight."

After a walk through two separate wings, Baurus turned into a bedroom. Inside were three people wearing yellow-and-black CrimeSolve uniforms, standing around a frilly mauve-and-mahogany bed with a body lying on it.

Kadin had investigated homicides for six months, but still the sight of a dead body made bile rise in her throat, even when there was nothing grisly about the scene. The slim-but-curvy form of blond bombshell Coelis Crest might have been sleeping for all the visible physical damage. But something about seeing the lifeless form of someone Kadin had seen in life—at least in films—so many times disturbed her.

Dahran didn't seem to notice the body. He stared at the man with the shiny "lead detective" star badge on his yellow-and-black jacket. "Varell Clout," said Dahran. "Fancy meeting you here."

"Dahran White." Clout's voice held as much menace as Dahran's did. Clearly, the two had interacted on cases before.

Judging by the glower on his face, Kadin knew Dahran wasn't about to take the lead on this case any time soon, so she figured she'd better. "You moved the body. I thought she was found in the closet."

Clout turned to look at her, although Kadin decided that *ogle* was a better word to describe the way he took in her form. "You finally got yourself an aide, did you, White? The girl's not bad, but I bet you could have done better."

Dahran looked about ready to punch Clout when Baurus stepped between them. "The girl is the lead investigator on this case. Thank you for your assistance, but it will no longer be necessary."

Clout smirked. "And how do you plan to solve a murder with no evidence from the crime scene?" He pointed to the camera his colleague held. "Jumper here's got all the clicks. And your girl looks sweet and all, but I doubt she can solve a real crime."

Now Baurus looked like he wanted to slap the smile off Clout's face, but he held himself back. "I'm sure she'll manage just fine."

"Baurus." Kadin noticed Clout's eyebrows go up at the familiar way she addressed the duke. "He's right. We need the information in those clicks, especially if Lady Beatrin won't cooperate." She turned to Clout. "I'm willing for us to work together on this. I'm sure my boss, Detective Caison Fellows, will be able to smooth out any jurisdictional issues."

"Caison Fellows is your boss?" Clout chuckled, though Kadin didn't see what the joke was. "Well, then, little lady, I suppose we can share the case with you, at least for tonight. Where would you like to begin?"

CHAPTER 4

"WHY DID YOU TELL CRIMESOLVE you were the lead investigator on this case?" Dahran hissed as they proceeded back down the hallway toward a pair of rooms Baurus had set up for interrogations. Jace and the forensic analyst from CrimeSolve had remained with the body, and Clout and the other detective from CrimeSolve engaged Baurus in terse conversation. "You're not the lead investigator. You're an aide."

"I didn't tell them that!" Kadin whispered back. "Baurus did. At least it made Clout willing to work with us. Well, it did once I dropped Fellows's name."

"That's another thing," said Dahran.

Phew. He thinks the way Clout reacted to Fellows's name was weird too. Maybe together we can figure out why.

The look on Dahran's face, however, was anything but conspiratorial. "Why are you on such familiar terms with the duke? You think he cares anything about you? He's a duke, for Deity's sake, and you're... you."

So much for "Kay, you're amazing." "Are you seriously jealous of a duke? Believe me, I'm well aware that he's practically royalty, and I am... not."

"You don't see the way he looks at you?"

Kadin glanced at Baurus, and as if Dahran's words cued him, Baurus turned and met her gaze. The light that shone in his eyes said he wanted to stare at her all day.

She broke the stare, and Baurus went back to looking where he was going. *I can't believe I mean anything to him. Royalty-commoner dilemma aside, we hardly know each other. So what if he brings out emotions in me no one else does? The urge to argue with Dahran is not a* good *emotion.*

"I notice you don't care about how Clout looked at me." *What was that I was just thinking about not arguing with Dahran?*

Dahran dismissed her complaint with a *pff*. "Please. Clout was just checking you out. That's normal. It's not like he has any intentions. He's married."

That shut Kadin up. *Does Dahran really think Baurus has intentions toward me?* The thought made her heart flutter in a way that felt half like nausea and half like amazement. She had never sought wealth or a title, and the thought of obtaining them made her stomach churn, but the idea of Baurus himself wanting her filled her with a strange kind of nervous elation.

Because he likes me for me, not for who I pretend to be... He brings out the worst in me—the difficult, argumentative side I try so hard to hide. And he still likes me?

Don't be ridiculous. He wants you to solve a murder for him, not marry him. But even that was impressive. For as long as Kadin could remember, society—largely in the form of her grandmother and then Octavira—had instructed her to get married. Solving crimes had never entered the picture as a legitimate, long-term option.

Kadin barely avoided bumping into Clout as she noticed the entourage had stopped.

"I think you can tell most of your guests they may leave," said Clout. "We've got a list of their names and will be in touch in a few days."

"Who are we planning to question?" Kadin asked then

mentally kicked herself for sounding so weak. She spoke again in a stronger voice. "We want to speak with Philindra Dixie and Mandrick Pane before they leave, as well as Duchess Beatrin, of course."

Kadin wanted to smack the smirk of Clout's face, though judging by Baurus's expression, he might beat her to it.

"Who exactly did you think was in this room, Miss Stone? We at CrimeSolve are not amateurs, after all."

Kadin chose to ignore the implication that detectives from Valeriel Investigations were amateurs. "We'll take Dixie first, and you can talk to Pane."

Clout's bushy eyebrows rose. Kadin knew she was giving him what he wanted—to talk to the alleged lover first—but Kadin suspected any real leads would come from the best friend.

Clout opened the door in front of him, and Baurus led Kadin and Dahran into the next room.

"I'll send in Philindra, and I guess send everyone home," said Baurus. "Let me know if you need anything."

"Thanks!" Kadin gave him what she hoped was a professional smile, but from the way he blinked and smiled back, she had come off as friendlier than she intended.

Baurus clicked the door shut behind him, and Dahran glared at Kadin. "See? What was that about?"

Kadin looked anywhere except at Dahran, which meant gazing about the opulent sitting room she found herself in. The carpet was a fluffy white, and she wondered if the room was never used or if the servants worked day and night to keep it that pristine color. Considering the lack of dust, she suspected the latter. The wallpaper featured a red-and-gold pattern that matched the brocaded chairs and loveseat.

"He just thinks I'm a good detective because I helped him out on that case a few months back." Kadin wondered

36

if her words counted as lies if she put enough effort into believing them.

Dahran set his jaw. "Caison Fellows solved that case."

Kadin had to hold back an amazed laugh. Dahran had been in the room with her when she'd solved the case. *Why is he always undermining my abilities?*

Trinithy's advice on similar situations ran through her head. *"It's not about you, Kadin. It's about him. He needs to feel like the man in the relationship, and you need to stop taking that away from him."*

"Well, it doesn't matter what Baurus says or wants," said Kadin. "What matters is what I want." *And there you go, making it about you again.*

Dahran didn't seem offended. He had that same smile she'd seen on her doorstep earlier that night. "And what do you want, Kay?"

Not you were the first words that popped into her head, but she knew they were the wrong answer—wrong if she wanted to keep that smile on Dahran's face, wrong if she ever wanted to get a husband who could get her out of Tobin's house.

The trouble was Kadin hated to lie, and somewhere deep in her gut, she knew this was exactly the wrong time to do so. If she lied now and told Dahran she wanted him, she could never take it back. She would marry him and have 2.5 children and be stuck with him for the rest of her life. With that possibility glaring her in the face, she couldn't find the breath to answer him.

A timid knock at the door interrupted them, and all the air she couldn't manage to inhale came out in a *whoosh.* "That must be Philindra Dixie." Kadin moved toward the door, smoothing her skirt as she went for want of anything better to do with the nervous energy that had gathered in her hands in the last minute.

Out in the hallway stood a woman with long black hair and brown eyes that had probably looked smoky when she'd put on her eye makeup earlier that evening. As she stood before Kadin, Philindra Dixie appeared more like a splotchy raccoon. Kadin hadn't recognized the name when Olivan had mentioned Philindra, but upon seeing the woman, Kadin remembered the actress from a film she and Dahran had gone to about a month before.

"Miss Dixie." Kadin made her voice as soothing as she could. "Please come in. My name is Kadin Stone, and this is my associate, Detective White. We have a few questions for you."

The girl—Kadin couldn't help thinking of the waifish, vulnerable-looking film star as anything else—shuffled into the room, her eyes on her feet. Her bearing was so different from that of the femme fatale Kadin had watched in the film that she had to wonder if this meek, terrified Philindra was the real person hidden behind the camera or if grief had dulled her spirit.

Or if both of them are just performances on different stages.

Kadin led Philindra over to the loveseat and sat in one the chairs, motioning that Dahran should do the same. Dahran didn't seem to notice, as his gaze was glued to the beautiful film star, and not in a manner Kadin would describe as professional.

So Baurus can't look at me with any interest, but Dahran can drool over the first eligible film star to cross his path? Kadin felt an unattractive frown crinkling her brow and reminded herself to stay calm. *It's different. Philindra Dixie is beautiful and famous. Who could help staring at her?*

After a few seconds of silence, Dahran started and sat down in the chair next to Kadin's. "Do you know why we've asked to speak with you, Miss Dixie?" Dahran asked.

"I thought... I mean, I heard... I thought someone said that Coelis... that Coelis..." Black tears welled up in Philindra's eyes then trailed down her cheeks, leaving more chalky black-and-red stains on her dusky complexion.

"I'm sorry." Dahran's voice held a level of compassion he reserved for interrogating witnesses he wanted to keep at ease. "Coelis Crest is dead."

Philindra's mouth opened in a silent scream, and she buried her face in her hands. "She can't be dead! She can't! I mean, I hadn't been able to find her for a while, but I just thought—" Philindra stopped and looked up, as if realizing other people were in the room. She sniffed, took a deep breath, and sat up straight, her face a serene, mascara-covered mask.

This is the act, which means that the grief is real—unless she's playing a very complex game.

"Miss Dixie, it's very important you tell us what you thought," said Dahran. "Did you see Miss Crest disappear with someone? Another party guest, perhaps?"

A burst of laughter escaped Philindra, but she shook her head and resumed her stoic demeanor. "Detective, I assume you've never been to an Imperial Gala because commoners are not welcomed here. No one wanted to talk to Coelis, Mandrick, or me, much less disappear with one of us."

"Really?" Dahran made a note on his pad then raised an eyebrow at Philindra. "It seems to me that a lot of nobles might see a pair of actresses at their party as little better than the help with one useful skill in their repertoire."

Kadin wanted to gasp at Dahran's crude implication, but she had her own detective's aide mask to keep up.

While Dahran hadn't broken Kadin's calm, he had certainly broken Philindra's. "Coelis wasn't like that!"

"Really?" Kadin hadn't known Dahran could pile so much disbelief into one word. "Then what was she like? Where did you think she was, Miss Dixie?"

"I thought she'd gone home!" Philindra wiped tears away from her eyes, her movements as incensed as her words. "I figured she'd gotten tired of being snubbed and propositioned and went home!"

"That seems unlikely to me," said Dahran. "Why wouldn't she tell her best friend, who she came to the party with, she was leaving? Would you do such a thing, Miss Stone?"

Kadin couldn't quite keep the pained look off her face. Not only had Dahran botched this interrogation in the worst way imaginable, he was bringing her into it. *I've got to salvage this interrogation, though Dahran's not going to appreciate my not siding with him.*

"Miss Dixie, perhaps you can tell me more about your relationship with Miss Crest," said Kadin.

"What are you, good cop?" Philindra glowered at Kadin. "He insults me, and you try to calm me down?"

I am good cop, thought Kadin, *in the sense that I actually am a good cop who can conduct an investigation without insulting a witness so thoroughly that they don't want to talk to me.* But she couldn't say that, nor could she apologize for Dahran right in front of him.

"I know our methods may seem unorthodox to you," said Kadin. "But I promise we are trying to do whatever we can to find out who killed Miss Crest. She was your best friend. You knew her better than anyone. If anyone knows who might have wanted to kill her, it's you."

Philindra hid her shaking hands behind her back. "I'll tell you," she said to Kadin. "But he has to leave."

Kadin turned to Dahran, hoping against hope he'd behave out of character and acquiesce to Philindra's request. Though his face remained neutral, his neck had tensed, and Kadin knew Dahran was going to rant at her when all this was over.

"I don't think you understand how this works," said Dahran. "We ask the questions, and you answer them if you want any hope of justice for your friend. Besides which, I'm the real detective here. She's just an aide."

"Fine." Philindra stood. "Then I guess we're done here."

Dahran whipped out his card and waved it in Philindra's

direction. "Call us if you actually feel like assisting in your friend's murder investigation."

Kadin hurried to catch up to Philindra as the actress rushed to the door. "If you wouldn't mind waiting in the hallway for a few minutes, the other detectives would like to talk to you as well."

Philindra gave Kadin a pained look as she exited the room.

As Kadin made her way back across the room to Dahran, she kept her eyes cast downward and wondered what she should say to him. Sometimes, when she didn't work with him for a while, she forgot what a terrible detective he was.

Do you really want to be dependent on this guy's skills for a paycheck for the rest of your life? she asked herself, too frustrated at the poor outcome of the interview to immediately chastise herself for the uncharitable thought and remind herself of Dahran's virtues.

She raised her gaze to meet Dahran's and suspected that the anger in her eyes matched his. "What was that?" she asked.

"I know, right?"

Kadin felt the anger rush out of her, and confusion took its place. *He's agreeing with me about his own incompetence?*

Dahran stood up, nearly knocking over the brocaded chair behind. "How dare she ask to talk to you and not me!"

Oh. Ohhh. He thinks I'm angry on his behalf. That's... that's probably good.

"I'm the detective here!" Dahran formed his hand into a fist and punched his chest. "That should be obvious from the fact that I'm the man in the room, and you're just a woman. You're lucky I let you tag along on this case without Fellows's permission!"

Heat rose to her face, and her own hands longed to form

41

fists at her sides. *How dare he! Just a woman, indeed! I'm perfectly capable of solving cases, and we both know we wouldn't even have this one if Baurus hadn't wanted me here. But of course, Dahran's delusional mind has made it all about him.*

"These female 'Entertainers...'" Dahran made air quotes around the word. "They're getting above themselves, thinking women can do whatever they want because being famous lets them violate the laws. But those laws exist for a reason!"

Kadin felt the bite of her nails in her palm and knew she had to calm down. If she exploded, not only would she would lose any romantic progress she had made with Dahran, but he would probably also report the incident to Fellows. She wasn't a hundred percent sure Fellows would fire her—he did seem to like having a competent aide—but she couldn't risk it. So she took what felt like her hundredth deep breath of the evening and sat back down in her chair. She was trying to calculate what to say when the door swung open behind her and banged against the wall.

"I was not having sex with Coelis Crest!"

Kadin didn't know whether to be grateful for the interruption or appalled at its content. She turned around to see a man so handsome he must have done some modeling before becoming a film star—which Kadin knew for a fact he had. Mandrick Pane's dark hair, blue eyes, and perfectly symmetrical features had brought him fame in the glossies before he appeared opposite Coelis Crest. Kadin had seen enough of his films to know his acting better suited the glossies.

Also, he was apparently not sleeping with Coelis Crest.

"Mr. Pane." Dahran also looked taken aback by the actor's declaration. "Please, come in and have a seat. We have some questions for you."

Mandrick snorted, but he did cross the floor, turn a chair around, and straddle it.

My chair, thought Kadin, but rather than argue about it, she settled into the loveseat. Much to her chagrin, Dahran settled down next to her instead of taking the empty chair.

"You want to know if I was sleeping with Coelis like those two morons one room over," said Mandrick. "I wasn't."

"Do you have any proof of this, um, lack of affair?" Kadin hated the way she stumbled over her words, but she wasn't used to people discussing things like sex so openly. Also, she disliked having Dahran's leg pressed up against hers while she was trying to interrogate someone. It was unprofessional.

"Proof." Mandrick barked out a laugh. "How do you prove you didn't have sex with someone?"

Now who's the rotten detective? "Well, an autopsy can certainly attest to Miss Crest's virginity."

"I wouldn't be surprised if it did," said Mandrick. "Coelis was always more interested in her career than in any man."

"And you resented that?" asked Dahran.

"Nah." Mandrick stretched out his legs and flexed his feet. "Nah. It was Coelis's business who she did or didn't screw. The glossies liked to pair the two of us up since I usually hung out with her and Philindra. Coelils is the classic beauty, of course. She's the one everyone's supposed to be in love with. But I've always had more of a thing for Philindra."

Dahran arched an eyebrow. *He's skeptical. And I'm not.* Both Mandrick and Philindra insisted that Coelis wasn't the type to sleep around, and while it might seem like a lie to protect her reputation, Mandrick at least was aware that an autopsy would prove it if they lied.

"When did you notice Coelis was missing?" asked Kadin.

Mandrick shrugged. "Didn't. At least, not until the Oriole broad started screaming about a dead girl in her closet."

Kadin smiled a bit at Mandrick's casual reference to the oh-so-respectable Duchess Beatrin. *Not that she was very respectable when I saw her this evening. Maybe it's her night for not rising to her station.*

"Then where were you at the time of the murder?" asked Dahran.

"We-ell." Mandrick rubbed his jaw. "Tell me, how confidential is what I'm telling you?"

"There are no confidences in a murder investigation." The words of Kadin's teacher came back to her. *"Anything a suspect says that can help you get to the truth is fair game."*

"I assure you, we operate with the utmost discretion," said Dahran.

"Though if anything you say becomes evidence in a trial, we cannot promise it won't come to light," Kadin felt the need to add.

"So Philindra and I got to talking about how we'd probably never be invited to another Imperial party, and this house probably had dozens of empty bedrooms. We thought it would be the perfect opportunity to, shall we say, couple in all the luxury life had to offer."

Kadin called upon all her experience as a detective and as Dahran's girlfriend to avoid wrinkling her face in disgust. The idea of having sex—Mandrick's words to describe his lack of actions with Coelis, if not his actual behavior with Philindra—in someone else's bed, even a seldom-used spare room bed, appalled her.

The heat of Dahran's leg pressed closer to hers, and she glanced at him. His eyes held a lascivious glint. *Oh, Deity. He thinks it's a good idea. Does he actually think I would...* She felt the truffled potatoes she had eaten with dinner roll in her stomach, and she was unable to hide a visible gulp.

Mandrick winked at Dahran.

Deity, they think I'm flustered because I like the idea and am too proper to say so.

"Well." Kadin stood up, grateful to no longer feel Dahran's leg against her own. She held out her hand to Mandrick and smiled for all she was worth. "We thank you very much for your time, Mr. Pane. I trust you will be available should we have further questions?"

"Of course." Instead of shaking her hand, Mandrick brought it up to his lips and kissed it. "Do enjoy the rest of your evening."

Oh, Deity. He thinks I'm rushing him out so Dahran and I can disappear somewhere in the house and have sex. I wonder if I would get fired if I vomited on his shoes.

Kadin stared at her blank notebook page as Mandrick said his goodbyes to Dahran. She didn't want to see any innuendo that passed between the two men.

These interviews were a complete waste of time. I didn't get anything. She focused all her attention on writing "Mandrick Pane having affair with Philindra Dixie, not Coelis Crest" until the door clicked behind Mandrick and Dahran's shadow loomed over her.

"So!" The pitch of Kadin's voice was high enough to be considered a squeak. "That was some pair of interviews! I think we got some very useful informa—"

"Kay."

"Hm?"

Dahran put his finger under her chin and raised her head until their eyes met. "Mandrick makes a very valid point about the facilities this residence has to offer."

"Right." Kadin's breathing became heavier, and she feared Dahran would interpret it as unbridled lust rather than the actual mix of terror and loathing that coursed through her veins. "That."

For the second time that night, Dahran's face came nearer to hers, and she knew she would have to suffer through another one of his kisses. She needed to figure out a way out of anything worse than kissing.

"Well, um..."

The door burst open, and Kadin jerked away from Dahran.

"Oh, thank the Deity!" she couldn't stop herself from saying.

Dahran gave her a confused look, and the interruption gave her enough presence of mind to give him a reassuring smile before she turned to see Baurus, Jace, and the three CrimeSolve men standing at the door.

Baurus looked ready to hit something. "Are you quite finished?"

Kadin felt heat rise to her face, but she wasn't sure if it was anger or embarrassment. *Baurus DeValeriel doesn't have any right to be angry at me for kissing my boyfriend.*

"The investigation is ongoing," she said with as much dignity as she could muster. To the CrimeSolve men she added, "I'll have detective Fellows contact you first thing Monday morning."

Kadin let Dahran leave the room first, and as the group paraded back down the hallway, she found herself next to Jace. "What did you get off the body?" she asked.

Jace put a finger to his lips and nodded toward the CrimeSolve forensic analyst. "I don't want to say until I've got a better picture of what's going on. I'll put something together for you on Monday." Jace opened his mouth and looked like he wanted to say something else then shook his head.

"What?" asked Kadin. "Is it about the case?"

"No, and it's none of my business. It's just..." Jace nodded at Dahran. "What do you see in that guy?"

Dahran had virtues. Kadin knew he did because she had listed them out for herself several times that evening. Yet somehow none of them were coming to mind at this moment.

"Ask me Monday."

CHAPTER 5

KADIN GOT HOME SO LATE on Saturday night—or rather so early Sunday morning—that her brother, Tobin, let her sleep in and miss church, much to Octavira's annoyance. When Kadin finally did wake up, she had to call Olivan and fill him in on all the details of the case, as she had promised she would, and as soon as she got off the phone with him, Ralvin called and wanted the scoop as well.

"So I don't think anyone suspects Baurus this time around, at least," Kadin finished up telling Ralvin. "But honestly, I don't know who to suspect. No one at that party had a motive for killing Coelis Crest."

"Well, that's good, I suppose," said Ralvin, "that Baurus isn't in trouble again, I mean. I'm sorry he brought you into the whole ordeal."

"Honestly, I don't mind. Solving murders is my job."

"True, but somehow I doubt Baurus—"

"Kadin Stone!" Octavira interrupted whatever Ralvin planned to say about his cousin. "Are you going to be on the phone all day, or are you actually going to help me with some of the housework?"

Kadin leaned out of the kitchen to see Octavira in the dining room with a pile of bedding in her arms. She didn't look much like she was prepared for housework in her white floral dress and three-inch heels, but then she never did.

"I'd better go," Kadin said to Ralvin. "Don't worry about me. I can handle Baurus."

That got a laugh out of Ralvin. "No one can handle Baurus, but you're welcome to try. I'll talk to you soon." There was a click on the other end of the line.

Kadin hung up, and by the time she emerged into the dining room, Octavira had headed upstairs, presumably to check on the children and make the beds. Kadin headed into the living room, where a number of papers and books lay scattered across the java table.

Kadin sorted through the papers first, some days-old to-do lists of Octavira's and a few bills. Kadin sorted the bills into paid and unpaid, and the latter pile made her cringe. She knew her brother got along all right on his salary, but she wished he allowed her to contribute more to the household expenses.

Most of the books were Tobin's medical journals. He always liked to keep abreast of the most recent research in his field. They were numbered, so even though she understood none of the topics in them, she could put them on the shelf in the proper order. Two of the remaining three books were scenic photograph books that belonged on the java table, but the third puzzled Kadin.

A surgery textbook? Why do we have this? Tobin's a primary care doctor, and he hasn't needed textbooks in years. She flipped it open to check the publication date. Maybe it was left over from his medical school days, though she couldn't imagine why he would have pulled it out. *Maybe he needs to consult on a surgery case?*

As she flipped through the books, she noticed the words "Property of the Valeriel City Library" stamped on a number of pages. She continued to flip through the pages, not knowing what she was looking for until she reached the end. When she got to the checkout pocket at the back, she read the name the library had released the book to: Octavira Stone.

I didn't know Octavira was interested in surgery. And that's unfair of me. I never thought of Octavira as interested in anything other than being a wife and mother, but of course, she has interests of her own.

Kadin returned the book to the java table. *Well, at least now I know what to get her for her birthday on Thursday.*

Monday morning, Kadin arrived at the office early enough to make java for the team, as was her custom. She tried not to think of Baurus as she poured the water into the machine and flipped it on, but she thought of him every time she brewed java. After all, he was the one who had helped her learn to make the beverage six months ago—and had provided the Astrevian grounds that had won her back into the good graces of the homicide department after her first botched attempt. Then after she had solved his case, both he and his fancy java had disappeared back into the upper echelons of society, leaving everything as it was meant to be. But that version of "meant to be" didn't allow him showing up in her living room on Saturday night.

He respects me as a homicide detective. Kadin poured Detective Fellows's java and carried it back to their adjoining offices. *And he needed a homicide detective. That's all.*

She placed Fellows's java on his desk at took a seat at her own. She pulled the cover off her typewriter and wheeled in a fresh sheet of paper on which to formalize her notes from Saturday night, except as she stared at the blank white canvas, she found she didn't want to commit any of her and Dahran's interrogation debacle to writing.

A knock sounded at the door, and Kadin glanced up,

grateful for the interruption, at least until she saw the woman who had interrupted her unpleasant memories.

Leslina Wolfsbane was more aptly described as striking than pretty. Her curly brown hair framed her face in a fashionable enough do, but her face needed more makeup to sharpen its hard angles. Trinithy had offered more than once to show Leslina how to do up her face in a more pleasing way, but Leslina had always turned her down, though if Kadin were being honest, Leslina's refusals probably had as much to do with Trinithy's mocking tone as Leslina's lack of interest in makeup.

"What brings you up from the call center?" Kadin said and instantly regretted it. Leslina would no doubt take that as a dig, since Kadin had worked in the call center before she had won the detective's aide position over Leslina. *Not that I really care if I offend Leslina. She's always gone out of her way to antagonize me, and I have no idea why.*

"Oh, haven't you heard? I'm not in the call center anymore." Leslina's eyes narrowed slightly at the corners before she said the words. "I would think that Trinithy or Olivan would have told you, but I guess you're not as close as you used to be, what with you having so much work to do as Caison Fellows's aide."

Leslina was no doubt referring to the fact that prior to Kadin, all of Fellows's aides had been hired for their looks rather than any detecting skills. Kadin, too, had been hired because of the effort she put into her appearance, but Fellows had also come to respect her as a detective. These days, her job really was a lot of hard work.

Leslina's words didn't sting for the reason she intended them to, but they hurt all the same. Kadin wasn't as close to Trinithy as she used to be, simply because she didn't sit next to her in the call center day in and day out the way she used to. And keeping Ralvin's secret had put a wedge between Kadin and Ollie that she couldn't quite breach.

Still, she would have thought one of them would have told her Leslina got a new job. Angry with Kadin or not, both of them were incurable gossips.

Hurt was the only explanation she could give for the words that came out of her mouth next. "Oh, congratulations! Did you get married?"

Of course Leslina hadn't gotten married. She had no interest in getting married. Leslina wanted to become a detective's aide more than anything in the world. She complained all the time about being lumped into the category of women who sought a husband above all else, and she always glared at Kadin when she did.

"No, silly! I got a job as a detective's aide in the robbery department!" Kadin had to give Leslina credit. She almost sounded as though she wasn't offended. "So maybe we'll be working together next time there's a robbery-turned-homicide!"

Kadin could hear the subtext: "And I will solve the case before you do, proving once and for all that I am the smarter of us."

"That'll be great!" A flash of fear burst through Kadin's chest. She realized Leslina might try to steal her job.

I have nothing to worry about. I did better in our detective's aide class than she did, and I've got six months of on-the-job experience. Yeah, but Leslina's got something I don't: the desire to be a great detective. All I want is a husband who will support me.

Leslina smirked as if Kadin's fears were written all over her face, which, Kadin admitted, they probably were. "Just headed off to get my routine bloodwork." Leslina referred to the mandatory drug testing all women employees took to prove they were not on birth control pills. "Shouldn't be that hard. I mean, you passed it."

Kadin sniffed, suddenly feeling angry rather than threatened. *It's one thing to imply I'm a rotten detective. It's another to say I should be a Class D!*

Fortunately, Detective Caison Fellows chose that moment to come into the office, sparing Kadin the need to respond to Leslina's taunt.

"Good morning, sir!" Kadin plastered her obligatory greeting-the-boss smile on her face as the older, balding man brushed past her. "When you have a minute, I'd like to discuss a case that came up over the weekend."

Fellows stopped and turned around. "The Crest case? Warring filled me in. I'll take care of it."

Interesting that Inspector Warring was the one who talked to him about it, thought Kadin, referencing the head of the homicide department. *Dahran said he was going to talk to Fellows directly, but I guess he decided to go over Fellows's head.* Kadin stopped herself before she had an uncharitable thought about her boyfriend.

"Yes, sir. I can be available to discuss it at any time. I have a few leads—"

"Don't worry about it, Miss Stone," said Fellows. "I can handle the Crest case. You focus on the Mook case and the Tiara case."

"Sir, if this is about what happened during the interviews—"

"Is my java in my office, Miss Stone?"

"Yes, sir." Kadin knew when she had been shut down. *It's fine. It doesn't really matter if I'm the one who solves the case, so long as it gets solved.*

As Fellows headed back to his office, Kadin stifled a groan as she realized Leslina had been privy to the conversation. "Don't you have a blood test to get to?"

"I do." Leslina fluffed her hair. "Have a good rest of your day, java girl."

Kadin laughed to herself as Leslina sauntered out of the office. If Leslina thought she wasn't going to be the robbery department's new java girl, she was about to learn otherwise.

Kadin pulled out her notes on Mook, a Merchant who had murdered his father for the inheritance money.

Leslina can be as competitive as she wants. Most of the time, we're just there to certify evidence. Kadin hated to admit it, but sometimes, she found detective work boring. The Coelis Crest case, though, had all the makings of a real investigation. *Too bad I won't be involved in it.*

CHAPTER 6

"I CANNOT BELIEVE YOU DID NOT call me!" A petite blonde wearing a pink, full-skirted dress appeared at Kadin's door as she packed up for the evening.

"Sorry, Trinithy," said Kadin, even though she was not entirely sure what she was apologizing for. "I take it Ollie spilled the beans about Coelis Crest."

"What?" Trinithy's mouth formed a perfect pink "o" as she flopped down in the chair opposite Kadin's desk. "Ollie knows? When I had to read about it in the paper like a plebian?"

Kadin stopped wondering how Trinithy always found lipstick that exactly matched the shade of her dress and sat up straight. "It's in the papers already? What did the papers say?"

Trinithy's voice took on a tone of ghoulish fascination. "Oh, only that Coelis Crest was found dead during Duke Baurus's party. And there was a statement from the duke saying you were on the case, so it would be solved in no time."

All the blood rushed out of Kadin's face. "He mentioned me by name?" *Deity, what will Dahran and Fellows think if the* Tribune *claims I'm in charge of the investigation?*

"No, silly." Trinithy brushed aside Kadin's words with

a wave. "He said 'the most talented detective in Valeriel,' which, of course, has to be you. You solved his whole ordeal last year."

That... is surprisingly discreet of Baurus.

Trinithy bounced up and down in her chair. "Anyway, we are going out tonight, and you are going to tell me everything."

"I can't tell you everything. There's such a thing as need-to-know. Besides, I have a date with Dahran tonight." Kadin found herself hard-pressed to determine whether she would rather spend the evening listening to Dahran blather on about race cars or fending off Trinithy's questions about a case Kadin wasn't even involved in anymore.

Trinithy cooed. "Well, I can't possibly come between you and your dreamboat. Where is he taking you? Someplace horribly romantic?"

Thank the Deity, no. "We're just going to check out the new club on Kendrey Street." *Where it will hopefully be too loud for anything even remotely resembling a proposal.* "Nothing romantic at all."

Trinithy's face lit up. "Excellent! Then we can join you!"

"We?" Kadin didn't think Trinithy was seeing anyone at the moment, but keeping track of her romantic entanglements required more attention than Kadin was usually willing to give, which might have explained why the two women weren't as close as they used to be.

"Me, Ollie, and Vinnie, of course! You apparently told Ollie everything—traitor—but Vinnie's going to want to hear, too! Besides, I said I'd go out with them tonight before I found out I needed to get your scoop."

Kadin opened her mouth to protest, but she knew it was a losing battle. She decided to change the subject instead. "I don't know why you're upset with me for keeping secrets when you didn't tell me about Leslina's new job."

Trinithy waved a dismissive hand. "No one cares about

Leslina and her stupid job. She's out of both of our hair now, and thank the Deity for that! No one wants her greasy brown mess anywhere near my lovely locks."

"And what lovely locks they are." Dahran appeared in the doorway and gave Trinithy's curves an appreciative once-over. "Looking good, Trinithy."

Trinithy preened and fluffed her hair. "Why, thank you! I was just telling Kadin about how wonderful it would be if we could go out with you two tonight. It's been so long since we talked."

Kadin pulled her purse out of her desk drawer and slammed the drawer shut a little harder than necessary. She could count on one hand the number of times Trinithy and Dahran had spoken, and most of those interactions had been as long and satisfying as the one Kadin had just witnessed.

But I guess I don't want Trinithy to tell him the real reason she wants to tag along.

Dahran gave Trinithy a small bow. "Always happy to have another lovely lady around." He glanced at Kadin. "Though of course none are as lovely as my lady."

Kadin bit the inside of her cheek until it hurt—and until she stopped herself from pleading too much work to go out that night. "Great! Let's go!"

The club was not as crowded as Kadin had hoped it would be, which meant they had no problem finding a table, and the music and conversation stayed at a low enough level that she couldn't plead a headache after an hour or two.

"This place is not making my top ten list." Olivan slid into the round booth after Ralvin, who pressed in closer to Kadin to make room.

"Aw, come on, they just opened," said Ralvin. "Give them a chance.

Olivan harrumphed, but Kadin knew he would acquiesce

to his boyfriend's wishes. *There go my chances of getting out of here early due to Ollie-boredom.*

Trinithy slid into the other end of the booth next to Dahran. She leaned in close and put her hand on Kadin's boyfriend's arm. Kadin might have been jealous if she didn't know that flirting came as naturally to Trinithy as breathing—and that Trinithy was just pumping Dahran for information.

Or if you actually liked him.

"So, Dahran," said Trinithy, "I hear you're involved in the Coelis Crest case. You simply must tell us everything."

Dahran laughed, pleased at the attention. "Well, I can hardly tell you everything. I haven't solved the case yet."

Trinithy giggled, a noise Kadin found more calculated than genuine. "But you can tell me what you do know."

"Trin, he can't." Kadin intended her voice to sound apologetic, but it came out sounding more annoyed. "We can't discuss an ongoing investigation."

Trinithy pulled back from Dahran and pouted at Kadin. Kadin couldn't help noticing that the pink of her dress clashed terribly with the bright-red vinyl of the seat cushions—really with the black, brown, and red decor of the entire club. "I don't want to know anything really secret. Just, what was the duke's house like? Did you meet anyone famous?"

"Come on, Kay," said Dahran. "We can give her something."

She's manipulating you, you dolt! But of course Kadin couldn't say that. "The duke's house was very nice," she said instead. "Lots of marble columns and red carpets. His entry hall was a giant ballroom full of Imperials dressed for a gala." *And waiting to go home so they didn't have to be in the same house as a dead body.*

Trinithy kept her lower lip stuck out, clearly disappointed with Kadin's description.

"We met Philindra Dixie and Mandrick Pane!" Dahran spoke in a rush.

Of course, he had to one-up me, which I have to admit wasn't hard.

"Oooh." Trinithy bounced a bit and flashed her golden eyelashes at Dahran. "What were they like in person?"

Sad, thought Kadin. *Angry. Confused. The same as anyone else right after a friend has died.*

"Larger than life," said Dahran. "It was like a film come right off the screen. Pane in particular made you wish you could have his life." He gave Kadin a sly wink.

Kadin did her best to smile then felt a hand on her leg. She automatically reached out to slap Dahran's hand away when she realized it had come from her other side. She hesitantly touched the offered fingers, and Ralvin twisted his hand to give hers a comforting squeeze. He and Olivan had been conversing about something else, but Ralvin had apparently paid enough attention to Kadin to realize she was uncomfortable. Her smile became a lot more natural after that.

"Hey, hey! Look who it is!" Olivan stood up and waved his hands in the direction of the door.

Kadin glanced toward the entryway and was surprised to see Jace and a blond woman Kadin recognized as his wife, Joelle. Jace gave Olivan a puzzled look at first, but then his gaze met Kadin's, and he nodded and headed over in their direction. Trinithy, Olivan, and Ralvin stayed focused on Jace as he approached, and for a moment, Kadin thought Dahran was as well. Then she realized Dahran was staring at Joelle.

Kadin took in Joelle's too-short skirt, low-cut top, and abundance of makeup and wondered if Dahran found her attractive. *She's kind of pretty but so trashy. I didn't think he was into that. Deity, I hope he doesn't ever want me to dress like that.*

Jace and Joelle perched themselves on the stools opposite the round bench of the table.

"Fancy meeting you here!" Olivan was at least half in love with Vinnie, by all indications that Kadin could muster, but even love couldn't kill Olivan's crush on Jace. She had to wonder if Olivan had somehow orchestrated this group of people.

That's ridiculous. Trinithy invited herself on my date, and there's no way even Ollie could have foreseen that. Probably.

"Dear, who are these lovely people?" Joelle's tone was sweet, but something poisonous lay beneath the innocent words.

"Oh, these are my coworkers." Jace gestured to them each in turn. "Olivan King. Kadin Stone. Dahran White, and Trinithy Gold."

He knows my name! Trinithy mouthed to Kadin.

Jace had the dignity to ignore Trinithy's less-than-subtle excitement. "I'm afraid I don't know you," he said to Ralvin.

"Vinnie Royal." Ralvin held out a hand, which Jace shook. "I'm with Ollie."

"Jace Combs, and this is my wife, Joelle."

Joelle hadn't taken her gaze off Kadin since Jace had said her name. "So you're Kadin Stone," said Joelle, now that there was a break in the conversation. "I've heard so much about you."

Heat rose to Kadin's cheeks as everyone turned to look at her. Since Joelle had just met everyone at the table— and Kadin thought it unlikely that Joelle was secretly best friends with Octavira—no one could doubt the source of the information.

Jace, for his part, had the decency to look embarrassed. "I haven't said that much about her."

"Oh, please." Joelle picked at something imaginary on her top, drawing everyone's attention to her breasts—well,

Dahran's attention, at least. Jace seemed inured to his wife's charms. "Not a day goes by that I don't hear about how grateful you are that Kadin Stone has joined the homicide team. 'Finally there's someone competent I can talk to,' you say."

Kadin froze, the sudden drop in her temperature a stark contrast to the heat she could all but feel rising off of Dahran as his temper rose. Joelle's less-than-off-the-cuff statement wasn't Kadin's fault, but she doubted Dahran would see it that way.

Joelle continued as if oblivious to the emotions flickering across the table. "At first when he started up about it, I assumed you had to be a man. Isn't Kadin a boy's name? But then I caught onto the female pronouns."

Lie, thought Kadin. She didn't know why Joelle would lie about something like that, except that Joelle's priority for the evening had become humiliating Kadin.

Before Kadin could say anything to attempt to salvage the situation, the first few chords of a Dawban Steel song belted out from the speakers. Kadin tried not to cringe. She had a strong distaste for Steel's music after an unfortunate run-in with him at one of Olivan's parties.

"I love this song!" Trinithy grabbed Dahran's arm. "And since I don't have a date, you have to dance with me!"

Under ordinary circumstances, Dahran would have made a token effort to dance with his girlfriend instead, but she suspected he was still smarting from Joelle's comments on his detective skills. Thus, Kadin was not surprised when Dahran accepted Trinithy's demand and headed off to the dance floor with her. What did take Kadin aback was the spiteful, amused glance he tossed back at her before he disappeared into the crowd.

Joelle pouted in her husband's direction. "I want to dance too."

"Have fun," said Jace. "You know I don't dance."

"Fine." Joelle stood up. "I'm sure plenty of people will be happy to dance with me."

Judging by the look on Jace's face, Kadin thought Joelle's attempt to make him jealous didn't have the desired effect. She spun on her spiked heel and trounced toward a group of men on the other side of the room.

"Shall we?" Olivan held out his hand to Ralvin, who took it, leaving Kadin alone at the table with Jace.

Kadin's mouth went dry as she tried to think of something to say. Inviting him to dance seemed like a poor idea, given that he'd said he didn't dance. *"So your wife's a total sub-D,"* also seemed like a poor conversation starter. She almost resorted to talking about the weather when Jace said, "Mind if we talk a little shop?"

"Not at all." Kadin heard the relief in her own voice. She wondered if it was wrong that homicide was the topic she found easiest to talk about these days. "Though I warn you, if this is about the Coelis Crest case, Fellows has told me in no uncertain terms to stay out of it."

Jace's fingers made little circles on the table between them. "Really? That's odd. Does he usually tell you to stay out of cases?"

Kadin raised a shoulder then let it drop. "Not usually. Occasionally. I think, this time, it's because Dahran and I bungled the initial interviews so badly."

The corners of Jace's mouth turned upward. "I find that hard to believe."

"Oh, believe it. I haven't alienated that many witnesses in all the time I've been a detective's aide, which, admittedly, has not been that long."

Jace's smile widened. "This is about the Crest case, but don't worry. I won't tell Fellows I consulted with you."

Kadin offered her own smile. "I won't tell, either."

"So as expected, the body got transferred to the

CrimeSolve lab, but I was able to get enough samples to do a preliminary tox screen."

"And?"

"Nothing." Jace sat back in his chair and let out his breath in a *whoosh*. "I can't find a single thing that indicates foul play. There are no marks on the body and none of the obvious drugs in her system, not even alcohol. It's as though her heart just stopped."

"That doesn't make any sense. She's younger than me." *Was younger than me. Always will be younger than me, I guess.*

"Oh, believe me, I know. I'd like to get to the body and do a full autopsy, but that's not going to happen. I'll talk to Fellows about at least getting the autopsy report from CrimeSolve, but I don't hold out a lot of hope there."

"So maybe it wasn't murder," said Kadin. "But if not, why hide the body? I suppose she could have died, and her friends could have gotten scared that they would get in trouble, but they really seemed—"

Kadin broke off when she saw the knowing look Jace gave her.

"No." She shook her head, slowly at first then more aggressively. "You do not think it was magic."

"I most assuredly do not think it was magic," said Jace. "That way lies madness and misery. Except..."

"Except the last time the Society of Mages came to Valeriel, there was a string of unexplained murders. And we know they're back. You think it was Herrick Strand." *Please, Deity, don't let Strand be back. I don't know how to stop him.*

Jace shook his head. "Herrick Strand burned a hole in Queen Callista's windpipe, and she suffocated. Coelis Crest didn't suffocate. Her heart stopped."

Kadin didn't know which was worse, the idea that Herrick Strand was back or the idea that there were two murderer mages at large in Valeriel. "There are still lots of possibilities other than magic. You said yourself you could only do a preliminary tox screen."

Jace slumped back in his chair. "You may be right. Get Fellows to get me the autopsy report from CrimeSolve. Then we'll see."

CHAPTER 7

"VALERIEL INVESTIGATIONS. DETECTIVE FELLOWS'S OFFICE. Kadin Stone speaking. How may I help you?"

After what Kadin considered her second debacle-filled evening of the week, she was grateful to be back in the office. Work, she understood. Navigating the complex relationships of a variety of different friend groups all mashed into one place was a different problem altogether. The highlight of her evening had been that Dahran was still so annoyed about Joelle's comments that he didn't try to dance with her or kiss her good night. She supposed she should be concerned for the future of the relationship, but Dahran had gotten in moods like this before, and they hadn't had any lasting effect.

The worst part of the evening was when the dancing couples returned to the table having had so much fun with each other, they decided they wanted to repeat the experience on Wednesday. Kadin was surprised when Jace agreed, but she got the impression he gave Joelle whatever she wanted, at least so long as he didn't have to dance.

"Kadin!" She would have recognized the voice on the other end of the telephone anywhere, though she found herself a little surprised at how deeply it had ingrained itself in her psyche. "It's Baurus."

Kadin felt her heartbeat pick up a little. She wasn't sure if she was more terrified that the Duke of Valeriel City was calling her or excited that Baurus was. "What's up?"

"Just calling to check in on the case."

"Right. The case." Of course, this wasn't a personal call. He'd called her office number. Besides, he'd had six months to make a personal call and hadn't bothered, yet the minute his sister found a dead body, he was in her living room. She was a detective to him, nothing more, which should have pleased her because she was just an aide to everyone else. "The thing about the case is—"

"Don't tell me you don't have any leads." Baurus's deep voice took on a wheedling tone. "I know you can find anything you put your mind to."

"It's not that." Kadin moved her hand up to run her fingers through her hair then stopped herself when she realized the gesture would ruin her do. "Fellows has decided that he would be a better fit for the case. He's got me working on other investigations." *There. That was diplomatic.*

"Kay, I hired you." Baurus now sounded frustrated. "I need you to solve the case. As far as I can tell, Fellows is incompetent."

"Fellows is a brilliant detective!" The words came out automatically. If she were being honest, she thought Fellows's reputation as the best detective Valeriel Investigations had to offer spoke more to the incompetence of his colleagues than his talents.

Baurus snorted. "I've seen no evidence of that. I need you on this case. I can call Fellows. Or his boss. What's his boss's name again?"

"No, no, that's fine." She could not imagine how Fellows would react if the duke called Inspector Blaik Warring and told him that Fellows's aide had to be the lead investigator on a high-profile murder investigation. "I'll work on the case."

"That's my girl." Baurus's words held a beaming smile. "Let me know when you've got something." Kadin heard a click on the other end of the line.

Kadin buried her head in her hands. She couldn't believe she had told Baurus she would work on the case against Fellows's explicit orders. If she didn't work on the case, she would have lied to Baurus, and she hated lying. On the other hand, Fellows was a good boss, and she hated to go against his wishes.

But Fellows is only keeping me off the case because he doesn't want me to botch it any further. If I prove to him I can solve it, he'll have to admit he was wrong. Keep telling yourself that, Kay. When has Fellows ever admitted to being wrong? The truth is, you want to be on this case. It's a real mystery, and it'll impress Baurus.

She picked up the phone and dialed the personnel office. "Ollie? Are you busy? I need your help."

An hour later, Olivan and Kadin were in Olivan's green sedan, headed out to the suburbs.

"Explain to me again why you needed me to track down Coelis Crest's parents for you." Olivan turned on his blinker and switched lanes. "Aren't you, like, detective's aide extraordinaire? Can't you find anyone and anything?"

"Well, you know..." Kadin almost cringed at the singsongy quality in her own voice. She was such a terrible liar. "Your records of famous people are so much better than mine. I thought you could find them more easily than I could. Part of being a good detective's aide is having good sources."

"Mm-hm." Olivan navigated around a curve. "And I'm going with you instead of Fellows or White because..."

This time Kadin did cringe. "All right, all right. Dahran and I messed up the original interviews pretty badly, so Fellows doesn't want me anywhere near the case."

Olivan took his eyes off the road long enough to beam at Kadin. "I can't believe you, of all people, are going against your boss's orders. I'm so proud of you."

Kadin rubbed her forehead. She was not proud of herself. "Well, the thing is, Baurus really wants me on this case. And it's a lot easier to gainsay Fellows than Baurus."

Olivan let out a squeal. "I still cannot believe you're on a first-name basis with the duke of the city. It's like my greatest dream ever."

Well, you're on a first-pseudonym basis with the king, but I can hardly tell you that." "Anyway, I couldn't do any research in the office without Fellows finding out, so I outsourced it to you. He might still think I'm doing interviews for another case."

"Kadin Stone. Did you lie to your boss about your whereabouts?"

"No!" The denial was out of Kadin's mouth before she could consider that she might also be lying to Olivan. "I may have used some creative language to hide my true intentions, however."

Olivan shook his head. "We'll make a rebel out of you yet." He glanced to his right and took the exit ramp out into the town of Clover.

As soon as they got off the highway, they were surrounded on both sides by rows of near-identical houses, differing only in the color of their siding and shutters. Each one was surrounded by a white picket fence. Some had autocars parked in the driveway, and one had two children playing in the yard with a barking dog.

This is it, thought Kadin. *This is the life I'm supposed to want—that I do want.* She tried to imagine living in this ordinary-ideal neighborhood with her own washer-dryer and dishwasher, and the dream felt somehow empty.

That's because you've gotten used to the excitement of homicide investigations. Life out in the suburbs would be much better—and much safer. She'd been lying so much lately, to Fellows, to Olivan, to herself, that she wasn't even sure what the truth was anymore.

Olivan pulled up to one of the houses, a white one with pretty blue shutters and a matching roof and door.

"You called them to say we were coming, right?" asked Kadin.

"Yes, though I'll never understand why I'm doing your job for you." Olivan turned off the car and opened the door to get out.

"Because you're a good friend." Kadin opened her own door and stepped out onto the sidewalk. "A good friend who is dying of curiosity about this case."

Olivan flashed Kadin a grin. "You are so right about that."

They walked up to the blue door and knocked. A middle-aged woman with graying blond hair and red-rimmed blue eyes answered the door. Based on the family resemblance, Kadin assumed this had to be Coelis Crest's mother.

"You must be the detectives," Mrs. Crest said. "Do come in."

She led them through a foyer, where pictures of Coelis at all ages adorned the wall. The pictures from the past few years, though, seemed to be movie posters and newspaper clippings, rather than family portraits or candid photos.

At the end of the hallway lay a spacious living room with plastic-covered floral furniture. A man with dark-brown hair and a mustache sat in one of the armchairs. His skin was distinctly tanner than either Coelis's or his wife's, and Kadin didn't see the family resemblance between him and the film star at all.

"I don't see why we need to talk to them." Mr. Crest

glowered at Olivan and Kadin. "We already answered all that other detective's questions."

"Now, dear, don't be off-putting." Mrs. Crest kissed her husband's cheek and sat in the other armchair, leaving Kadin and Olivan to sit on the sofa. "They're trying to find out what happened to poor Coelis." Mrs. Crest's words were light, but the way she tripped over them at the end let Kadin know that the mother was trying not to cry. "Can I get you detectives something to drink? Some java?"

Olivan brightened. "That would be—" He caught the glare Kadin gave him. "Terrible. I mean, unnecessary. Definitely don't want any java."

"I'm sorry to bother you again, Mrs. Crest," said Kadin. "You must have had many detectives contact you already."

"Oh, no, just the one," said Mrs. Crest. "Detective Clout, I believe he called himself. And it's Mrs. Dove."

"Oh, I apologize." Kadin mentally cursed Olivan for not giving her this information he must have had. "I assumed... Was Coelis Crest a professional name, then?"

"Not at all. I used to be Mrs. Crest," said Mrs. Dove. "Coelils's father died when she was just a little thing, Deity rest his soul. I married Robbin here a few years after that. I felt like Coelis needed a father figure in her life."

"Ah, of course." Kadin couldn't blame Coelis's mother for finding another husband. The laws that prevented women with children from working also provided a stipend for raising the child, but a working husband brought in much more income. "You're sure Detective Clout is the only investigator you've heard from? You haven't received a call from Detective Fellows?"

"Are you calling my wife a liar?" Robbin Dove stood up and took a threatening step toward Kadin. "I don't need some chit of a girl coming into my house and playing at being a detective while we are grieving."

Kadin swallowed. *He's angry from grief. That makes sense.* She tried to tell herself not to let this big man scare her. She'd faced any number of belligerent witnesses. Trouble was, usually when she did, she had Fellows backing her up.

Olivan shot to his feet. "My name is Detective Olivan King, and I don't appreciate you talking to my aide that way. I am letting her take the lead on some of the interviews in this case because I felt like it would be a good experience for her. I trust you will treat her with the same respect you would me."

Kadin did her best to keep her face neutral in the face of Olivan's lie.

Dove sniffed, but he stepped back. "Not sure I appreciate you using my stepdaughter's murder as a training exercise."

"Now, now, dear," said Mrs. Dove. "I'm sure she's perfectly competent." She gave Kadin a reassuring smile. "Go ahead and ask your questions, dear."

Kadin gave Mrs. Dove a genuine smile. "I first wanted to say—"

"Too late," muttered Dove.

"That I am sorry for your loss. Coelis was a very special girl to a lot of people, but nowhere near as special as she was to you. I know this cannot be easy for you."

"Thank you," said Mrs. Dove. "She is—was—always my baby. But I have to admit that we hadn't seen her for some time before her death. After she moved into the city and became famous, she never had time for her poor parents."

Tears formed in the corners of Mrs. Dove's eyes, and Kadin found herself wanting to respond in kind. Her own parents had died when she was six years old, and she would do anything to see them again. It always pained her to hear about people ignoring their parents.

"Do you know anything about her current friends? Did she have any enemies?" asked Kadin.

Mrs. Dove deflated. "Nothing other than what's been in the papers and the glossies. I read everything I could about Coelis's life. There was a woman who lost out on a part to Coelis, but all her interviews seemed good natured about it."

"Tell me her name, anyway," said Kadin. "It might lead to something."

"Of course. Dominga Easter was the name."

"Did Coelis have any problems at home before she left?" asked Kadin. "I know it's painful to talk about, but if there was a reason she stopped coming home, it might relate to her death." Kadin shifted her eyes to Dove for a moment. He glowered at her but did not say anything.

"Not that I know of," said Mrs. Dove. "She always promised me she'd come home soon, and then something would come up. She was very dedicated to her work."

"I understand," said Kadin.

"May I ask you a question?" asked Mrs. Dove.

"Of course."

"The other detective, he wouldn't say. The papers said nothing, either. But I wanted to know. How did Coelis die? Did she suffer?"

Kadin had heard this question any number of times in her six months as a detective's aide, so she had a ready answer waiting. "I can't give out the details of an ongoing investigation, but I can say that she didn't seem to suffer." Kadin didn't always offer that last bit, but in this case, she believed it was true. Coelis had looked remarkably peaceful in death, and if her heart had given out, either by magic or other means, her death was likely quick and painless.

"I think that's all the questions I have for you right now," said Kadin. "Please call Valeriel Investigations if you think of anything else that could help us."

"Absolutely, we will. Thank you so much."

As they headed out of the house and back to the car, Ollie said, "Well, that wasn't particularly helpful, was it?"

"It didn't seem to be. But you never do know."

CHAPTER 8

THAT EVENING, KADIN STOPPED OFF at the bookstore to pick up a birthday present for Octavira, confident that, for once, she had purchased something her sister-in-law would like better than a scarf. As she stepped out of the bookstore, she couldn't help thinking of another building a few blocks over, one whose proprietor could help her in her investigation. The shop, if it could be called that, was in a bad part of town but just a block over. She would probably be safe. She found her feet walking in that direction.

She walked up to the purple, dirt-covered building with the words Magick Shoppe etched in the window. There was one magic expert in Valeriel City, and he lived and worked here. Kadin took a deep breath and opened the door. Dust-covered shelves of curios and knick-knacks filled the room. Daimon Gates told the average passerby these were magic items, but he had revealed to Kadin that none of them were. He kept his real magic collection in the back, believing it to be too dangerous for the average consumer.

"Mr. Gates?" Kadin stepped into the shop. "Are you here?" Silence met her ears—or not quite silence. She thought she could hear the sound of voices coming from the back.

She crept slowly among the shelves, trying not to feel like a damsel who was about to have a monster jump out at her. *Honestly, why doesn't Mr. Gates dust these shelves? Unless he likes living in the setting of a horror film?* From what she knew of the man, he just might.

As Kadin approached the back room, she was surprised to see the door open. Gates usually kept the door closed to keep the magic items inactive. She heard a female voice coming from inside the room.

"—didn't get dug up after a hundred years to sit around in a dusty shop doing nothing!"

"And I have not been hiding from the Society of Mages for the past twenty years to suddenly go on a killing spree!" Kadin recognized that voice as Gates's. "Besides which, I don't trust you."

"Because you think I'm a mage or because I'm red?" The woman's voice was strident and insistent. Kadin had rarely heard a woman talk back to a man that way.

"Because you're a homicidal psycho."

"Don't be ridiculous. I can't kill anyone without someone else pulling the trigger."

"You can be either very annoying or very persuasive, as evidenced by the fact that I am still listening to you instead of shutting that door."

At that point, Kadin had approached the room enough to see inside. She saw Daimon Gates, a tall, thin man with graying dark hair, standing over the much cleaner row of lighted curio cabinets in his magical back room and rubbing the bridge of his nose. There was no woman in the room.

Kadin cleared her throat, and Daimon looked up at her. He seemed relieved to see her, though she wondered if that was more to do with the conversation he appeared to be having with... himself?

"Kadin Stone." Gates stood up straighter as he said her name. "It's been awhile."

Kadin felt heat rise to her cheeks. "I'm sorry, I—"

"Don't be. I don't want you here." He sighed and dropped his shoulders some. "Shut the door."

Kadin obeyed then glanced about the room, partly from curiosity about whether any new magic items had arrived since she had been there but mostly to try to identify the source of the female voice. Could mages become invisible? The woman had identified herself as a red mage, whose specialty was destroying things. Kadin didn't see how destroying anything could make one invisible.

The only noteworthy thing she noticed in the room was a new item on display: an antique pearl-handled revolver put on a prominent pedestal in the middle of the room. The silver of the gun looked clean and polished for something over a century out of date, but Kadin supposed it was magic. The metal tag labeling the item simply said "Xanidova."

"Were you here for a reason?" Gates asked Kadin.

She realized she had been rude again, this time in a probably less welcome way. She made herself meet his brown eyes. "I'm here because I have questions about magic."

Gates snorted. "I'm not going to answer them. I told you to stay away from magic, and I meant it."

"I did!"

Gates crossed his arms.

"I tried. But this latest case I'm working on seems to involve magic again, and I need to know more about it."

Daimon grunted. "Let someone else solve it."

Kadin let out a humorless laugh. "I tried that too. Unfortunately, when the duke of the city thinks you're the only person who can solve his crimes, it's difficult to say no."

"Duke Baurus DeValeriel? You should stay away from him too."

Now it was Kadin's turn to cross her arms. "I'm sorry. Are you my father now, to tell me what to do?"

Gates raised a finger. "I'm—" He cut himself off and dropped his hand. "Never mind. You're right. Ask your questions. I don't promise answers."

Kadin considered him for a moment, wanting to ask more questions about that near outburst, but she decided to continue with the task at hand. "Last time I was here, you said there were three different types of mages: red, blue, and green. Red magic, the kind Herrick Strand had, destroys things. But what about blue magic? You said it was stopping magic. You said it could stop someone's heart. Were you telling the truth?"

Gates collapsed into a nearby chair and motioned that Kadin should do the same. "I'm not answering yes or no, but presumably, if one had the power to stop things, hearts would be included. But I might also add that any number of drugs—and natural causes—can have the same result."

Kadin sat down in the plush purple chair opposite Gates. "I know. I might be jumping to conclusions. I just—"

"Someone in the investigation?" asked Gates. "Have they seemed especially blue to you?"

Kadin frowned. "No? I mean, Philindra Dixie was sad, but I wouldn't say that grief is the same as being blue."

A look that was equal parts disappointment and relief flashed across Gate's face. "Then perhaps you have not yet found your killer. Or perhaps you are simply unable to see them."

"How does one see magic? For that matter, how does one become a mage?"

"It is worth more than my life to give you that information, Kadin Stone. And it is better for you that you do not know. The Society of Mages likes to make examples of those who interfere with their business."

"People are dying, Mr. Gates. I can't let that go."

Gates closed his eyes and took a deep breath. "I know that, Miss Stone. I am doing my best to answer your questions in a way that does not put either of our lives in jeopardy."

Kadin frowned. "That's not particularly helpful."

"The best advice I can give you is to stay out of the Society's way. They'll come, and they'll go, and everything will be as it should."

"And how many people will die before that happens?"

"Not as many as you might think. But probably more than you're comfortable with." Gates got up and walked over to the door.

Kadin stood. "Even one is too many."

Gates inclined his head. "As I said, I know you won't stay out of it." He opened the door. "I want you to take Xanidova."

"What?" the female voice rose in the room again, and this time, Kadin was able to identify the source as the antique revolver she'd admired a few minutes previously. "I'm not going with her."

Gates walked over to the case and lifted the ject. "You wanted to fight mages. Miss Stone is fighting mages, and I would feel better if she had some measure of protection."

"Is that... does that ject talk?" asked Kadin.

"Yes," said Gates, at the same time that Xanidova said, "No."

Gates shook his head. "I dug Xanidova up on my last trip to find magic items. She's been itching to get outside ever since, and I think going with you is the perfect solution. I can trust her not to tell you too much."

"I can't walk around with a talking gun," said Kadin. "What are people going to say?"

"Nothing," said Xanidova, "because I'm not going with you."

"Nothing," said Gates, "because you're going to keep her in your purse and not tell anyone you don't trust completely about her."

"I cannot go with her," said Xanidova. "She's—"

"Silence!" Gates roared. "You will go with her. She wants the same thing you do. If you don't believe me, ask her."

"Fine. Point me at her."

Gates obliged, and Kadin found herself looking down the barrel of a ject.

"Do you want to destroy mages?" asked Xanidova.

Kadin shuddered. *And Gates thinks we want the same things?* "No. I just want to stop them from killing anyone else."

No one said anything for the longest moment, and Kadin had the impression she was being considered very carefully. She wondered if her lack of bloodthirstiness would make Xanidova order her trigger fired. She wondered if Gates would oblige.

"Okay," said Xanidova eventually. "I'll go with you. But I will tell you nothing. And don't think for one second that I trust you. One wrong move, and I'll find someone willing to put a bullet in your brain."

CHAPTER 9

KADIN SPENT A GOOD HOUR that night trying to get Xanidova to talk to her, but either the revolver didn't want to talk with anyone else in the house, or she didn't want to talk to Kadin. Nevertheless, Kadin found herself putting the ject in her bag the next morning. She told herself it was because she didn't want to see the look on Octavira's face if her sister-in-law found it, but the truth was that Kadin felt safer having a weapon on her person.

When she arrived at the office, Trinithy waited in her office, her eyes lit up like the endless row of clubs in the Nighttime District. "Kadin! You will not believe the news!"

Kadin placed her bag in her lower desk drawer, conscious of the weapon housed within. She wondered how detectives dealt with carrying jects around all the time. *Of course, they don't have to worry about their ject suddenly talking to everyone in the room.*

"Probably not," she said to Trinithy. "What's the big news?"

Trinithy leaned forward, the glint in her eyes turning malicious. "Leslina failed her blood test."

All thoughts of Xanidova fled Kadin's mind as she stared at Trinithy. "Leslina what? Are you kidding me?"

"Nope. Positive for birth control pills." Trinithy's voice

was somehow dramatic and singsongy at the same time. "She is now officially Class D and barred from ever working again."

Kadin hung up her coat on the rack next to her desk. "How is that possible? Leslina's wanted to be a detective's aide for as long as I've known her. Why would she mess up something like that?"

"Apparently, she was having an affair with one of the higher-ups here. I guess she thought he would cover for her, but he didn't!"

Kadin realized she was chewing on her lip and stopped. She didn't want to mess up her lipstick this early in the day. "Maybe he really wanted to marry her and thought this was the best way to get her to give up her dreams?" Kadin wasn't sure whether she found the notion romantic or repugnant.

"Nope!" The light in Trinithy's eyes sharpened to a razor point. "He's already married. She was his little trollop on the side, and now she's absolutely nothing."

Kadin's phone rang, and she breathed a sigh of gratitude. She wasn't sure how much longer she could listen to Trinithy's glee at another human being's suffering, even one as difficult as Leslina.

Kadin reached across the desk to grab the phone. "Valeriel Investigations. Detective Fellows's office. Kadin Stone speaking."

"Kay!" The voice, as it had the day before, made the hairs on her arm stand up.

"Baurus!" Kadin made an apologetic face at Trinithy and mouthed, *I have to take this.* Trinithy held her hands up in an *I understand* gesture and exited the office. "I take it this is about the case."

"Right, the case." Baurus snapped his fingers on the other end of the line, and Kadin wondered what he had been calling about if not the case. "How's it coming?"

"Well, I have some desk-side detecting to do this

morning, but I should be out conducting interviews in the afternoon. Just need to figure out how to get to Dr. Isidri Tell's office." In his research the day before, Olivan had turned up the name of Coelis Crest's doctor, and Kadin planned to investigate whether Coelis Crest had been paying him to hide any birth control usage.

"That's great, Kay. I know you'll solve this thing in no time! So I wanted to ask you—"

Kadin never found out what Baurus wanted to ask her because her boss's tuneless whistling sounded down the hallway, and she interrupted. "I'm really sorry, but I need to go now. Fellows is on his way."

"Aw, did you forget to bring him his java?"

Actually, yes, now that you mention it. "A java girl's work is never done."

"You're not a java girl," said Baurus. "And you should never let anyone treat you like one." He hung up.

Kadin hurried out of the office so that Fellows wouldn't have to ask for his java. He was never happy with her on mornings when she forgot.

"Ah, Miss Stone," he said to her as she brought the piping-hot java into his office. "Where are you on the Mook and Tiara cases?"

"I should have both of them to you tomorrow." She actually planned to finish both cases this morning, but she needed the extra time to work on Baurus's case. "May I ask where we are on the Cr—"

"You may not." Fellows gave her a stern look. "I told you to stay off that case, and I meant it."

"Yes, sir."

Kadin meandered back out to her desk and tried to focus on the Tiara case, but her mind kept wandering. She couldn't stop thinking about the ject in her bottom drawer, the lies she told Fellows, and the agony Leslina must be in. She told herself she was going to take a bathroom break, but she found herself continuing toward the elevator and heading to the Robbery department. From there, it wasn't difficult to locate the dark-haired young woman putting the last of her personal effects into a box.

"Leslina."

"Come to gloat?" Leslina dropped a picture frame into the box with a *clank*. "You're a little late. Trinithy already had her little call center friends up here laughing in my face."

"No, I—" *Why* am *I here?* "I guess I'm here to see if you need any help."

"Help?" Leslina spat the word. "You think I need your help? I need neither that nor your pity, Kadin Stone."

She's speaking from a place of anger and hurt. She doesn't mean it. But then Leslina always spoke from a place of anger and hurt, and she always meant it.

"I guess I just mean that I know you're hurting right now. And you don't have a ton of friends"—*Smooth, Stone*—"so if you needed someone to talk to—"

"I'm fine, thanks." Leslina did not sound very thankful. "In fact, the best thing about getting fired is that I finally have you out of my life."

Kadin felt something inside her snap. "You know what, Leslina? I don't get you. You call me stupid all the time, but then you go and get caught using birth control pills. You knew the rules. You knew what would happen if you got caught, and you knew a new job would come with a mandatory test, so you would get caught. Yet you did it anyway. So tell me, really, which one of us is the stupid one?"

Leslina's face turned red. "You are. It'll always be you because I'm at least smart enough to realize that this world isn't fair. And I try to change it. I try to fight it instead of being the good little girl everyone expects me to be."

"But you've lost everything!"

"Have I? Maybe. We'll see about that." Leslina hefted her box off the desk. "At least I won't spend the rest of my life chained to the likes of Dahran White. Have a nice life, Kadin Stone. I hope you get exactly what you've always wanted."

Kadin watched Leslina march out of the room and resisted the urge to run after her and apologize. Kadin knew better than to kick a woman while she was down, even if that woman deserved it, and suspected an "I'm sorry" would lead to another argument. With a heavy heart, she headed back to her office.

"Dahran?" Kadin knocked on the doorframe of her boyfriend's office. She hadn't talked to him since Monday, and the two-day reprieve felt like more of a relief than she wanted to admit.

"Kadin!" Dahran seemed happy to see her, which meant he had either decided Joelle's comments on Monday weren't her fault or decided to forgive her. Either way, she was grateful to see pleasant Dahran back.

Not that Dahran's ever particularly pleasant.

"Hey," she said. "I just wanted to let you know that I have to run out and conduct some interviews this afternoon, so I'll meet you at the club."

Please don't argue. Please don't argue. Please don't argue.

Dahran narrowed his eyes. "I'm not sure it's a good idea for you to be roaming around the Nighttime district on your own."

Kadin tried to laugh off his concern. "I'll be fine. I used to do it all the time before we got together." *Besides, I have a gun now.*

"Yes, well, it's all well and good to do that kind of thing when you're single, but you're mine now."

Kadin shuddered internally at his use of the word "mine." He didn't own her and should know better than to think he did.

"I don't like the idea of all those guys out there looking at you, thinking you're fair game."

Of course. He doesn't care about my safety, *just making sure no one lays a hand on his property.* Kadin almost kicked herself for the uncharitable thought. Of course, Dahran would be upset if something happened to her. *Because he cares about you or because he would see it as a personal insult?*

"Don't worry. I checked the autobus, and it stops right outside Divinity. I won't have any time for guys to bother me, and if they do, you'll be right there." Ordinarily, she'd ask him to come along on the interview to appease him, but she didn't want him to know she was working on the Crest case in case it got back to Fellows.

Speaking of... "Hey, Dahran, does Fellows have you working on the Crest case?"

"What? No. Why would he?"

"No reason. Just that you and I started the investigation, and he's keeping us both away from it."

Dahran gestured at the slew of papers on his messy desk. "You know I've got a huge pile of cases already. I don't really need one more. Warring gives me enough grief as it is."

Probably because you're a terrible detective. "Okay, well, see you at the club tonight?"

"I guess." Despite Dahran's grumbling, she doubted she'd be treated to a night away from his company.

She headed down the elevator to the ground floor. She considered stopping by to say hi to Olivan, but he'd already told her he had a lot of work to do that afternoon. "Real work," he'd sworn. Kadin had always been vague on when Olivan found time to do his actual job between his rampant celebrity page stalking and taking the afternoon off for mani-pedis—or in the case of yesterday, to drive her to an interview.

She'd made the decision to take public transit over to

Dr. Tell's office. The autobus should drop her off only a few blocks away. She simply had to wait for the number-thirteen autobus outside her office then switch to the number twenty-one at Market Street.

Before even one bus could come, a bright-red convertible with black leather seats pulled up in front of her with Duke Baurus sitting in the driver's seat, sunglasses over his eyes and crimson sleeves rolled up to his elbows. "Need a lift?"

Kadin hurried over to the passenger side door, but she didn't get in. "What are you doing here?"

Baurus lifted his sunglasses to look her in the eye. "You said you didn't have a lift to your interview."

"No, I said I needed to figure out how to get there, meaning I had to look at the public transit map. There's a big difference."

Baurus ran his hands over his arms as if to push up sleeves that were already above his elbows. "Well, I didn't have anything better to do, so I thought I'd make it easier for you."

"You know, it doesn't really make me feel better to know that the guy who rules the city doesn't have anything better to do than follow me around a routine murder investigation."

Baurus grinned, not looking offended in the slightest. "Hey, this murder investigation is a big deal for me. The body turned up at my party. My reputation is at stake."

A loud honk sounded from behind the autocar, and Kadin realized that the large number-thirteen autobus was bearing down on Baurus's car, which was parked in the autobus-only lane. With a quick look back at the autobus, which she knew she should take, she pulled open the door to Baurus's convertible and sat down.

As he pulled out into the main traffic lane, Baurus glanced down at her purse. "Is that a ject?"

Kadin pushed Xanidova underneath her wallet—where

she swore she'd placed her that morning—and zipped the bag closed. "No. Definitely not."

Dr. Tell's office was in the Merchant District, which surprised Kadin more than it should have. Generally, since the kingdom paid equally for all forms of medical care, people were assigned to the facilities nearest where they lived. Coelis Crest should have had a doctor near her apartment in the Nighttime district, according to most people's standards.

Of course, Coelis Crest was a rich and famous film star, and everyone knew that not all kingdom-funded medical facilities were created equal. The best ones were in the Merchant district, and Coelis Crest would have nothing but the best.

A woman with curly blond hair sat at the receptionist's desk when Kadin and Baurus walked in. "Do you have an appointment?"

Kadin walked over to the desk while Baurus walked over to admire the paintings on the wall. "My name is Kadin Stone. I believe my associate Olivan King called earlier. I'm an investigator with Valeriel Investigations, and I'd like to talk to Dr. Tell about Coelis Crest."

The woman *tsk*ed. "Such a shame what happened to that poor girl. She was so young and beautiful, sweet too. Always had a kind word for me when she came in."

"Did she come in often?" asked Kadin.

"Oh, every few months or so, though her last few appointments were on my days off," said the receptionist. "Dr. Tell did her routine bloodwork when she started on a new film. And she always passed, of course. She was a good girl, no matter what the glossies liked to say."

"Of course," said Kadin. "Can you tell Dr. Tell I am here to speak with him?"

"I'll tell him," said the receptionist. "But you know

doctors, always some emergency or other. You may have to wait a bit." The woman glanced up, whitening as she noticed Baurus for the first time. "Is that the duke?" she whispered.

Oh, Deity, how to answer that one? "That... is my chauffeur for the afternoon." Her words were true enough and didn't require her to explain why a duke was following her around on an investigation.

Kadin sat down on the edge of one of the waiting-room chairs, trying to look as dignified as possible. Baurus flopped down into the chair next to her.

I suppose when you're a duke, you don't have to worry about what other people think about your posture. She thought back to her interviews with other Imperials during the investigation into the queen's death. They had all seemed to care what people thought of their outward appearance. Maybe the outward relaxation was a Baurus thing.

"This guy's got good taste." Baurus pointed at the landscape he'd been admiring. "That's not the original— Bay's got that in the guest room she likes to stick me in out in Oriole—but it's a damn good copy."

Kadin shook her head and tried not to think what her brother Tobin would say about doctors making enough money to buy expensive art for their waiting rooms. *Something, something everyone should have equal facilities.* Then Octavira would say there was nothing wrong with making money off one's profession, and Kadin would feel bad for working in the for-profit service sector, and the whole rest of dinner would be awkward.

"You're frowning," said Baurus. "Thinking about the case?"

Kadin laughed. "No, thinking about my brother, actually. He's a doctor too, and he's not a huge fan of acquiring wealth. Probably why he keeps supporting me in spite of my total failure to find a husband."

Baurus spread out his hands. "What is it with women and getting husbands? My mother's the same way. Never seen her so thrilled as the day my sister married Frasis, and that guy's a total jerk."

"Yes, well." Kadin tried not to sound huffy but failed. "Most women don't have huge fortunes to fall back on, and we can't make enough money to support ourselves. No one's going to promote a woman who's going to run off and get married or become ineligible for employment any day."

"But that's the thing," said Baurus. "Bay did have a huge fortune to fall back on. There's no reason she should have had to get married, except that my mother threatened to disinherit her. You say it's about money and supporting yourself, but it's not just that."

Kadin had never really thought about it from the point of view of an Imperial before—and really, why should she? They were the rich elite, so far above her that she couldn't touch them, except she was now within arm's reach of a duke, and she'd spent over an hour on the phone with a king the other day. So maybe she should take their whole perspectives on marriage to heart.

"What is it, then?"

"It's this horrible norm ingrained in our culture that women can't be anything or do anything without a man, and it's perpetuated as much by women as anybody else. I once told my mother and Bay I was going to fight for women's rights in the Assembly, and the resulting shouting match could be heard from the next estate."

Considering how much space there was between Imperial estates, that was saying something.

"Seriously, Kadin, do you even want to get married?" asked Baurus. "I know you can't possibly want to marry that idiot you're dating, but even if you did. Is that what you really want? A white picket fence, two-point-five kids, and being completely dependent on someone else for everything?"

Kadin stared at Baurus. She didn't know what she was supposed to say. She expected Baurus wanted her to say what she actually thought, but *yes* and *no* stuck to the tip of her tongue in equal measure. *Yes, it's what I'm supposed to want. No, Deity save me, that sounds boring. Yes, it's what will keep me safe and secure. No, it's not really safe for my well-being to rely on one person.*

Baurus's hazel eyes drilled into Kadin's. "Because, Kadin, if you want to get married that badly—"

"Miss Stone?"

Kadin started away from the spell Baurus had her under.

"Dr. Tell will see you now."

"Excellent." Kadin rose, feeling dizzy. *I must have gotten up too quickly. All the blood rushed to my head.* That had to be it. It couldn't be a reaction to that conversation or a deep desire to know how Baurus planned to finish his sentence.

Dr. Tell's office was as elaborately designed as his waiting room. Judging by the gold-plated mahogany that made up the bulk of the furniture, Kadin thought the man's job paid well. That the tall, thin, balding man behind the desk wore a designer suit that would not have been out of place in the boardroom of Valeriel Investigations added to her suspicions. Since Kadin knew quite well the kind of lifestyle a doctor could usually afford in Valeriel, she had to assume that Dr. Tell's income was quite illegal.

Or maybe he's independently wealthy or something— became a doctor to give back to the community.

"Miss Stone." Dr. Tell stood and held out his hand to her, and she took it. She had to resist a shudder at the cold clamminess of his hand. "And your associate is..."

"Baurus DeValeriel." The duke held out his hand, seeming to take Dr. Tell's flustered response in stride.

"Don't worry," Baurus added with a wink. "She asks the questions. I'm just along for the ride."

"I see," said Tell as all three of them sat down. His tone said, *I don't see at all.*

Kadin supposed that a doctor who strove as hard as Tell to rise above his station wouldn't understand why a duke would be slumming it with a lady detective. Though, come to think of it, Kadin also wasn't entirely sure why Baurus was following her around.

"Well, then, Miss Stone," said Tell. "How can I help you today?"

"I understood you were Coelis Crest's doctor." Kadin hated the hesitant sound in her voice, but her questions were delicate, and she had no way of knowing how Tell would respond. "I don't want to put you on the spot or ask you to confess to a crime, but it's very important that we know Miss Crest's actual medical history, which is to say you have certified several times that Miss Crest was not taking birth control pills, and I need to know whether those documents were falsified."

Baurus snorted.

Kadin glared at him. "Something to say?"

"Just that of course he accepts bribes for falsifying those ridiculous birth control documents. He didn't get this rich on a doctor's salary." Baurus leaned forward. "Isn't that right, doctor?"

Kadin gritted her teeth. "I'm terribly sorry, Dr. Tell. My—"

She avoided having to put a name to her and Baurus's relationship when Dr. Tell interrupted. "His Grace is quite correct. A number of young women take birth control pills for a variety of reasons, not simply to avoid pregnancy. Regulation of the menstrual cycle is one. I am of the belief that we should not take choices away from women simply because they have a medical need."

"So you provide this service out of the goodness of your

heart?" Baurus managed to indicate the doctor's designer suit and expensive furniture with only his eyes.

"Well, a man has to eat," said Tell. "I don't see why I shouldn't benefit from the service I provide."

"And you only falsify documentation for women who have a medical need for birth control pills?" asked Kadin.

"Ah, well, not necessarily." Tell folded his hands. "You see, I believe in choices for women, including the choice to have sex when they choose."

"And Coelis Crest was one of those women whose choices you respected?" asked Kadin.

Tell sat back in his chair and steepled his fingers. "In a word, yes."

Today is apparently my day for people rubbing women's choices in my face. Is it really that hard to not have sex? I seem to have managed just fine.

"Do you have any evidence of these transactions?" asked Kadin.

Tell picked up a folder and handed it to Kadin. "Foreseeing your request, I took the liberty of printing out both the official results and the modified document."

Kadin glanced at the two papers, each dated two months ago. They looked identical to each other, except that one listed a positive result for the second of five tests.

"Five tests?' she asked.

"Ah, yes," said Tell. "There are any number of illicit new birth control products on the black market at any given time. The state requires testing for these five specific substances."

Kadin nodded. "Is there anything else you know about Miss Crest's medical history that might be relevant to the case?"

"Not that I can think of." Tell gave her a small smile. "Miss Crest did not so much as have the sniffles in all the time I have known her."

Kadin nodded and made a note. "And how long has that been?"

"I've been her sole medical provider for five years."

She still lived with her parents out in the suburbs then. Interesting that she would have needed the specialty services of someone like Tell even then.

Kadin stood up and held out her hand. "Thank you, Dr. Tell. You've given me a lot to think about."

Baurus and Tell rose as well, and Tell shook her hand. "You are very welcome, Miss Stone. I can't think of any other information I might have, but if you think of any further questions, don't hesitate to stop by."

CHAPTER 10

"SO WHERE SHOULD I DROP you?" Baurus asked as they headed back out to the car.

"Do you know where Divinity is? The club on East Street?"

"No. Should I?"

Kadin shook her head. "It's only the most popular club in the city, at least that we mere mortals can go to. But I guess you Imperials have your own clubs."

Baurus tilted his head to the side in acknowledgement. "If it's the most popular club in my city, maybe I should check it out."

"Huh, yeah, maybe sometime you should." Kadin actually thought that was a terrible idea. Divinity had the occasional Entertainer or Merchant come in—Ralvin was going to be there tonight, after all—but an actual Imperial would cause nothing but chaos.

Which was why Kadin was surprised when Baurus asked where he could park.

"Wait, what? You can't come in!"

"What? Embarrassed to be seen with me?" Baurus's grin said he knew exactly what kind of trouble his arrival at a mundane club would cause, and he was relishing every minute of it.

"Baurus, seriously." She could think of any number of reasons she didn't want him coming in, and none were related to the impending paparazzi storm.

First was Dahran. He would not react well to her showing up with another man, even one as out of her reach as the duke of the city. Second were Olivan and Trinithy, who would be certain to fawn over him in a ridiculous manner, assuming they weren't stunned into silence. Third was Joelle Combs. What if Baurus thought she hung out with people like that?

And finally, and probably most importantly, there was Ralvin, or Vinnie, as he would be calling himself. She had told Ralvin she would keep his worlds from colliding, and if she brought Baurus into the club, she would be doing the exact opposite of her promise.

But as Baurus pulled into a parking garage and wound his way around the too-full levels, she realized she had no control over the duke's behavior.

It's fine. Dahran will get over it. He's gotten over worse things. Ollie and Trin shouldn't embarrass me too much, and with any luck, Joelle will be dancing all night the way she did Monday. As for Ralvin, I'll just pray he's in bed with a cold.

Baurus held his hand on the small of Kadin's back as they approached the club. She should have told him to remove it, but she liked having it there. She wasn't a huge fan of crowds, and even though it was early enough that the line wasn't very long, she appreciated having someone to fend off any unwanted advances.

She was less pleased when Baurus insisted on paying her cover charge. She was not on a date with the duke. She had a boyfriend.

But wouldn't you so much rather be dating Baurus? came a voice from the back of her mind.

No. No, I would not. Her stronger, more controlled

thought drowned out the traitorous one. *He's a duke, and he's not interested in me that way.*

The entered the club, which even at this early hour was busier than Monday night's club had been at peak time. Kadin spotted Olivan, Trinithy, and Jace at a table across the room and waved. *Good. Ralvin's not here yet. Maybe I can head him off.*

Trinithy lifted her hand to wave at Kadin but stopped when she noticed her friend's escort. She poked Olivan, who had been deep in conversation with Jace, and Kadin had three pairs of eyes and three dropped jaws trained on her.

Might as well get this over with. She started toward the table, but before she could move more than two steps, Baurus tugged on her arm. She turned back to him, and he stepped forward. She found herself looking up at him, their bodies nearly touching, his fingers lacing through hers.

When he whispered, "Dance with me, Kay," she felt the warmth of his breath on her face.

She tried to step away but found herself mesmerized by the fascination in his hazel eyes as he studied her face.

"I should go say hi to everyone." Her mouth went dry.

"Aw, come on." Baurus's lips smiled as his gaze dropped to her mouth. "One dance. Then we'll both go say hi."

Dahran wouldn't like it. But as Baurus rubbed his thumb along her palm, she found it hard to think of Dahran.

"One dance," she found herself agreeing.

"Maybe two." Baurus's smile widened. Was it her imagination, or had he moved even closer?

"Baurus—"

Before she could agree to a second dance or tell him to forget the whole thing, though it was even odds which she would choose, a much rougher hand ripped her arm out of Baurus's grasp, and for the second time in as many minutes, she found herself spinning to face a man.

"What do you think you are doing?" Dahran's face was red. His nostrils flared.

Oh, this is not good. "Just dancing with Baurus," she said, though she knew there was no "just" about it. She would be a fool to think Baurus wanted an innocent, meaningless dance, though she was hard-pressed to determine exactly what he did want from a commoner like her.

"Just dancing with another man? Like you aren't my girl?" Dahran's jaw clenched, and Kadin saw a blood vessel pulsing at his temple.

Kadin opened her mouth to apologize but then caught a glimpse of Baurus out of the corner of her eye. *If I don't defend myself, Baurus is going to do it for me, and the last thing I want is Baurus and Dahran going toe to toe in a public place, or any place.*

"You danced with Trinithy the other night." She tried to sound reasonable. "I don't see how this is any different."

"How dare you talk back to me, you bitch?" Dahran raised his hand, and Kadin had just enough time to realize she was about to be backhanded when a large hand reached in and wrapped itself around Dahran's much smaller hand.

"Touch her, and you will be in for a world of hurt." Baurus's tone was quiet, but there was a menace there that spoke of the power of kings at his disposal.

Dahran ripped his hand out of Baurus's grasp, though Kadin suspected that if Baurus hadn't wanted to let go, Dahran would still be in his grip. "We'll discuss this later. And he won't be around to protect you." Dahran stalked off into the crowd.

A number of people stared and murmured around Kadin. *Just great.* "Let's just go over to the table." She kept her head down, definitely not looking at Baurus as she made her way across the club.

Kadin put her purse down on the table. "You all know Baurus." The words came out of her mouth in a rush. "Baurus, I believe you've met Jace, and these are Trinithy and Olivan."

Trinithy let out a high-pitched giggle, and Jace looked grumpier than usual. Baurus, for his part, remained cool and greeted everyone. Kadin expected Olivan to start peppering Baurus with questions, but instead, he grabbed Kadin's arm, and she found herself yet again being pulled in a direction she had no intention of going.

"Kay and I need to have a word," Olivan called over his shoulder. "We'll be right back."

He dragged her down the dark hallway that led to the bathrooms and dropped her wrist. "What were you thinking, bringing Baurus DeValeriel here?"

"I didn't bring him!" Kadin rubbed her arm. She'd definitely had more than her fair share of wrist-grabbing today. "He followed me. You try telling him not to do something he wants to do!"

Olivan crossed his arms. "Like make out with you in the middle of the dance floor at Divinity?"

"We did not... do that!" Kadin realized her voice was louder than she wanted it to be and lowered her volume. "He was just asking me to dance."

"That's not what it looked like from where I was sitting," said Olivan. "No wonder Dahran got so upset."

Kadin closed her eyes. She knew she should agree with Olivan, but she found herself saying what she thought instead. "Dahran is an asshole."

"Kadin Stone! Do you kiss your brother with that mouth?"

Kadin groaned. "Seriously, Ollie. No jokes now."

Olivan leaned back against the wall. "You know that I more than anyone am a perennial supporter of a woman finding herself a good husband. But seriously, if you dislike Dahran that much, maybe you should break up with him."

Kadin felt tears prick the corners of her eyes. "And then what? It's not like I have a long line of guys chasing me."

Olivan looked back in the direction of the club, and despite the wall in the way, Kadin knew he had zeroed in on their table.

"I cannot marry Baurus DeValeriel!" she hissed.

"Why not? He seems to like you, and everyone knows he's a rogue agent. I could totally see him marrying a commoner."

"And what kind of life would that be?" asked Kadin. "All of his friends and family would hate me for not being one of them, and it's not as if we could just go out like normal people. I'm surprised the paparazzi haven't already descended on us. In fact, they may have while we were back here."

"But you haven't thought about this at all." Olivan grinned.

"Speaking of poor relationship choices, where's your significant other?" Kadin had a hard time calling Ralvin anything but his real name, which made communicating with Olivan feel like a lie these days.

Olivan's face fell. "He's running late. And why do you keep calling it a poor relationship choice? He's rich and attractive. Someday, we're going to have beautiful children, and you'll feel bad."

"I've told you. He's a Merchant, and you're an Imperial-lover. Never the twain shall meet." Kadin sighed. "But I hope it works out for you. You know I only want you to be happy."

"And I you," said Olivan. "Oooh, I just had an idea! Want me to murder Jace's sub-D of a wife so you can marry him?"

"I think my wishes for your happiness would have to be put on hold while you were locked up in jail. But I appreciate the thought."

Olivan stood up straight and wrapped his arm around Kadin's shoulder. "Anything for you, my dear."

As they emerged back into the main club, Kadin noticed Dahran hadn't returned to the table. "I should probably go find Dahran and apologize."

"If you're sure that's what you want to do," said Olivan. "He was going to check his coat when he ran into you, so I'd look in that direction. I, for my part, finally have an Imperial who has to pay attention to me, and I'm going to ask him everything I've ever wanted to know."

You have an Imperial paying attention to you every day, and you have no idea. "Good luck with that. Baurus has no filter. You'll probably end up with more information than even you want."

Kadin headed over to the cloakroom and was surprised to see there were no attendants taking coats and handing out tickets. *That must have made Dahran even more furious. He hates it when serving staff don't do their jobs.*

She crept around past the check-in table. Dahran might have decided to hang up his coat without a ticket, though Kadin knew she would never do such a thing. What if they refused to give her coat back?

As she inched closer to the cloakroom, she thought she heard voices inside, which was odd. Had all the staff decided to hang up coats at once? And were they laughing?

I should leave before I get caught. But her detective's mind needed to solve this mystery, so she moved forward, taking tiny steps so as not to be heard, and when she finally rounded the corner to the cloakroom, she could not believe what she saw.

She recognized those two people, half-naked and pressed up against each other, making noises decent people didn't want to hear their neighbors make.

Dahran White and Joelle Combs having sex in the cloakroom at Divinity—while she was forced to watch.

Kadin couldn't breathe. She needed to get out of this stale club air, and possibly vomit, although not necessarily in that order. Creeping just as slowly as when she went in, she exited the cloakroom, reminding herself that it was unladylike to dry heave.

Dahran must have bribed the cloakroom staff to give them space, Kadin's numb mind thought. *That's why no one's there.* A small part of her was satisfied to solve the mystery, but the rest of her wandered like a zombie out of the club, ignoring the doorman's query as to whether she wanted her hand stamped.

After she had gulped down a few breaths of slightly cleaner city air, she felt a bit better, but her thoughts still raced. *Dahran's an asshole. I knew that. I said it to Ollie earlier. But I thought he was better than that. I'll go home. I'll just go home and sleep, and everything will seem clearer in the morning.*

As she stepped forward to hail a cab, she realized two very important things. First of all, she had left her purse inside the club, so she had no way to pay for a cab. And second, Ralvin was going to arrive at any moment, and when he walked into the club, his secret would be uncovered.

The first she could get around. She could ask the cabbie to wait outside her house while she ran in to get some money. She hated to do it, but she could. But she had promised to keep Ralvin's secret, so she didn't see that she had any choice but to sit down on the curb and wait for him to arrive so she could warn him about Baurus's presence.

Nobility of purpose aside, she had a hard time focusing on the crowd and looking for Ralvin's arrival. Her mind kept flashing back to Dahran's fingers in Joelle's blond curls, Joelle's heel digging into Dahran's leg, Dahran's—

She squeezed her eyes shut, trying to rid herself of the memory. She concentrated on the blackness behind her eyelids and willed that to be her entire world, which worked for a second until her eyelids started to hurt.

"Kadin?"

She opened her eyes to find Ralvin standing above her, a quizzical look on his face. "Hey, Ralvin."

"Is there a reason you're sitting out here on the curb?"

"You can't go in there. Baurus is here. He decided to follow me because..." She tossed her hands in the air, at a loss to explain the duke's behavior.

"Because he's Baurus." Ralvin sank down on the curb next to her. "And the reason you're looking for me through eyes closed so tightly you can't even see the sunset is..."

Kadin crossed her hands over her knees and buried her face in them. Even she couldn't make out the words that emerged from her lips.

"Pardon?"

"Dahran and Joelle were having sex in the cloakroom," she said, louder this time, but thankfully not loud enough that anyone but Ralvin could hear it.

"Ah." Ralvin reached over and rubbed her back. "Kay, I don't know Dahran that well, but does it really surprise you that he's cheating on you?"

Kadin rolled her head back. The sun had not quite set, rendering the sky a lovely purple. She thought it unfair that her night should be ruined so early, when only the barest hint of one of the crescent moons graced the sky.

"No," she said. "It doesn't. I just... I'm supposed to marry him. That's what everyone wants to happen. He wants it. Octavira wants it. My friends all want it. This is supposed to be it. I meet a handsome man with a steady job who actually likes me, and it's supposed to be a dream come true."

"Kay—"

"But somewhere along the line, it turned into a

nightmare, and I don't know what to do about it. All I know is I hate my life." Kadin hadn't thought of it in those terms before, but as soon as the words escaped her mouth, she knew they were true. "I'm tired of having to be what everyone expects of me instead of who I actually am."

"Believe me, I get it," said Ralvin.

A sarcastic "Do you really?" nearly made its way out of her mouth, but as she looked over at the dark-haired man sitting next to her, she realized that he probably did. After all, his actual life forced him into a role even more constraining than hers, that of a ruler of a nation that had very strict expectations of how its royalty should behave. Not that Baurus ever let that influence his behavior, but Kadin suspected that Baurus's wild streak put even more pressure on Ralvin to conform.

"Maybe you ought to take a page out of my book," said Ralvin.

Kadin gave him a sideways look. "I'm not creating some kind of alter ego for myself. The only thing I actually like doing is solving mysteries, and I'm not becoming some kind of rogue crime solver. Friends don't let friends become vigilantes."

Ralvin laughed. "I wasn't going to suggest that. I was going to say that maybe you should figure out what you want and make it happen."

"It's not that easy. I want to be a detective, but I don't want to deal with all the little digs I get every day when no one believes a woman can do the job. And I don't want to be a burden on my brother and Octavira."

"So start small," said Ralvin. "Break up with that jerk boyfriend of yours."

Kadin smiled a little at that. "You're right. I know you're right. It's only... What will Octavira say? What if Dahran decides to retaliate at work, and I get fired? There are a million ways this could blow up in my face."

"And what good will come of staying with him?" asked Ralvin.

Kadin closed her eyes and took a deep breath. "Nothing. You're right. Tomorrow, I'm breaking up with Dahran White."

CHAPTER 11

SINCE KADIN WASN'T QUITE BRAVE enough to go back in the club, and Ralvin couldn't go in anyway, Ralvin gave her a ride home. When Kadin entered the house, Octavira was frowning at the departing blue convertible.

"Where's Dahran?" asked Octavira. "Shouldn't he be giving you rides home?"

"Dahran and I broke up," said Kadin. "Or at least we're going to."

"What? Kadin, are you insane? He's a young detective! Someday, he could be making millions!"

Kadin had expected to quake in her heels at Octavira's chastisement, but since she had made the decision to break up with Dahran, the things she'd feared seemed trivial. "He was cheating on me. A million dollars isn't worth that."

"Well, while you've been off making poor decisions, the phone has been ringing off the hook. Some woman named Philindra keeps calling. She says she has urgent information for you regarding her friend's death."

"Philindra Dixie?" Kadin hurried over to the phone, or more specifically, to the notepad next to the phone where the family recorded messages. "Did she leave a number to call her back at?"

"Finally, after about the fifth time she called." Octavira's tone made it clear whom she blamed for the situation. "I told her you wouldn't be home until late, but she insisted on calling back every fifteen minutes for over an hour. During dinner time at that!"

Kadin ripped the top sheet, the one with Philindra's phone number written in Octavira's curvy script, off the notepad. She used the rotary to dial the numbers. "How long ago was her last call?" asked Kadin as the phone rang.

"I don't know, about an hour ago?"

Kadin didn't have time to respond to Octavira's snide tone because someone at the other end of the line picked up. "Miss Stone? Please tell me that's you." There was a note of hushed panic in Philindra's voice.

"It's me." Kadin was impressed at how efficient and professional she sounded. "How can I help you, Miss Dixie? You said you had some information about the case?"

A distant crash sounded from somewhere in Philindra's house. "I sent you a message," whispered the actress. "It should give you everything you need."

"Miss Dixie, are you in danger? I can send help!" Kadin rifled through the phonebook next to her telephone, looking for the Valeriel Investigations emergency line.

"It's too late for that now," said Philindra. "Just find justice. For both of us."

"Are you on the phone?" yelled a male voice on Philindra's end of the line. "Who are you talking to, bitch?"

"No one," said Philindra. "Just saying some good-byes. I love you, Mandrick." Kadin thought that last sentence was addressed to her, but she wasn't quite sure. Was Mandrick the man threatening Philindra? Kadin thought she recognized the voice but not from any film.

"Miss Dixie," Kadin said into the phone. "I'm going to hang up. I'm going to call for hel—"

Before she could get out the last "p," a loud bang

105

sounded at the other end of the line, and Kadin realized she had never heard a ject shot in person before.

"I'm going to call for help," she repeated, though she wasn't sure if it would do any good.

Grateful the starlet's domicile was a matter of public record, Kadin rushed as fast as she could over to Philindra Dixie's home. It took her the better part of an hour to get across town, and her heart sank when she saw the yellow-and-black crime-scene tape cordoning off the premises. She was surprised, but only slightly, to see a yellow-and-black CrimeSolve vehicle with red lights flashing parked in front of the lavish apartment building.

When the neighbors hear a ject shot, they call CrimeSolve.

Kadin wished she had a ject of her own with her, but she'd been kicking herself all the way over for leaving her bag—the bag with the talking gun in it—at the club. She could only hope that either Olivan or Jace had thought to grab it for her—without looking inside.

She pushed her way through the crowd gathered outside the scene and ducked under the crime scene tape.

"Whoa there, little lady," said the CrimeSolve man guarding the premises. "There's been a murder here. You're not allowed inside."

Kadin flashed her badge and was grateful to see Mason and Coterie, two Valeriel Investigations responders she recognized, heading in her direction. "I'm Kadin Stone with Valeriel Investigations. I called in the emergency team."

The CrimeSolve agent let out a chuckle. "Honey, the neighbors called us."

"And she called us," said Coterie. "She was on the phone with the victim at the time of her death."

The responder looked Kadin's floral dress up and down as if to say, *You don't look like a detective, sweetie*, but he stepped back and allowed her access to the building.

"If you're a witness, the detective will want to have a word with you." Kadin ignored his condescending tone and hurried up the stairs.

She didn't have to search to determine which apartment was Philindra's. There were only four doors per floor, and the first door on the left of the third floor was wide open. She followed the sounds of voices into what looked like a bedroom. The ivory carpet offset the mauve walls, and Kadin was sure the decor would have been lovely if every surface were not spattered with sticky red blood.

Lying on the floor was a very dead Philindra Dixie. Coelis Crest had looked like she might be sleeping, but the giant bullet hole in the middle of Philindra's forehead left no doubt as to the cause of her death.

Jace and Olivan were in the room, leaning over the body, Jace in studious examination, Olivan in morbid curiosity. Kadin had called Divinity and left a message for them to hurry over. She technically shouldn't have called Olivan, but she needed backup. Fellows didn't want her on the case, and she wasn't about to break up with Dahran at a crime scene. Also in the room were Detective Clout and his two associates she remembered from Baurus's estate.

"Ah, Detective's Aide Stone," said Clout. "Finally, someone with something resembling credentials decides to show her face."

"I told you, I'm a detective." Olivan's tone was laconic, as if he'd said the same thing five times, and it wasn't getting any less true. "I don't bring my badge with me when I'm out clubbing."

From the expression on Clout's face, he didn't believe Olivan's lie, but he wasn't confident enough to make a stink about it. "So tell me, Miss Stone. How did Valeriel Investigations come to be involved in this aspect of the case?"

"Miss Dixie called me." Kadin relayed the content of her phone conversation with Philindra. "I don't know what that last part meant. I thought I recognized the voice of the person in the room with her, but I didn't think it was Mandrick Pane. I think she didn't want her killer to know she was talking to a detective." *And she trusted me to pass one last message to the person she loved.*

"And this is why we don't let women do the detecting," said Clout. "She names her murderer to you, and you still can't solve the case. Most cases are open-and-shut, Miss Stone. We're just there to stamp the evidence."

As recently ago as yesterday, Kadin might have flushed at the chastisement, and maybe tomorrow, she would again. But after the day she'd had and the murder she'd audibly witnessed, she didn't feel ashamed of herself for having a different opinion.

"Why would she tell her murderer that she loved him?" asked Kadin. "I know if my boyfriend showed up with a gun in his hand, I wouldn't be speaking any words of affection to him."

"Who knows why women do the things they do?" said Clout. "She was probably hoping to stay his hand. She mentioned Pane by name, and he was at the site of the Crest murder. That's enough for me."

"That's circumstantial evidence at best, and you know it," said Kadin.

"Well, Miss Stone, if you wish to launch your own investigation, you're welcome to do it." Clout gave her a knowing smirk, though what exactly he thought he knew, she was at a loss to determine. He turned to Jace. "Is it okay if we take the body with us on our way to arrest Pane? I know cause of death can be difficult for some detecting companies to determine."

Jace glowered at him. "I think I can recognize 'bullet to the head' when I see it. Though you will, of course, send over the full autopsy report when you have it?"

"Of course, of course." Clout waved his associates out of the room and moved to follow them. "Painter will be up to collect the body in a moment."

After the CrimeSolve team left, Kadin found herself staring at Jace, who rushed to collect as many samples from the body as he could. Well, "rushed" was the wrong word. He took every sample carefully, but he moved with enough efficiency that she knew he was getting more than the average forensic analyst would in the time allotted.

He deserves better than Joelle. She wondered if she should tell him about Dahran and Joelle but decided against it. He probably already knew about his wife's proclivities, and she didn't want to hurt him further.

"Well, isn't this fun?' asked Olivan. "My first ever for-real murder scene!"

Kadin cringed. "Yeah, sorry about that, Ollie. I—"

Olivan waved a dismissive hand. "It's no biggie. It's kind of exciting." He let out a big yawn. "But now I'm tired, and this crime scene is just getting colder. What do you say we reconvene in the morning for a post-mortem." He snorted. "Apparently, literally in this case."

Jace glared at Olivan. "A woman is dead. Have some respect."

Olivan shrugged off Jace's chastisement, but he did settle down a bit.

"Hey, did either of you happen to pick up my purse?" asked Kadin.

Olivan and Jace exchanged glances, and unfortunately not ones that said, "We have no idea what you're talking about."

Kadin rubbed the bridge of her nose. "Who has my bag?"

The exchange of looks repeated itself, and it was Olivan who spoke first. "Duke Baurus."

Kadin didn't sleep well that night. Somehow, the idea of Baurus having her bag and her talking gun didn't sit well with her. She hoped Xanidova had the good sense to keep quiet around Baurus, but Deity even knew what talking guns thought.

The next morning, Kadin got to work as early as she could and left Fellows's java waiting for him before heading down to the morgue. No doubt the beverage would be cold by the time he arrived, but she didn't want to risk him yelling at her to stay off the case before she could talk to Jace and Olivan about it.

Olivan was already in the lab when she arrived. He had hoisted himself up on the steel counter, much to Jace's obvious chagrin. *Poor Jace. No idea how to deal with Ollie.*

"Morning!" Kadin greeted the pair of them. "So, Jace, how many dead body parts do you think you've left on that table right where Ollie's sitting?"

Olivan leapt off the counter so fast Kadin thought he might actually have seen one of those body parts. "Deity's sake, Kadin! Why'd you have to make me think about that?"

As Olivan made an elaborate show of brushing off his posterior, Jace mouthed, *Thank you* to Kadin.

"Why are we meeting in the morgue, anyway?" asked Olivan. "Not that I don't love seeing Jace's not-so-smiling face first thing in the morning, but couldn't we meet somewhere with a better smell?"

Jace rubbed his forehead. "Explain to me again why he's here."

"I need backup," said Kadin. "Fellows doesn't want me on the case, and I'm avoiding Dahran."

Olivan pointed at her. "Aha! I knew something happened last night! You completely disappeared, which meant Duke Baurus left way too early—"

"Probably because he was tired of your inane questions," muttered Jace.

Olivan stuck his tongue out at Jace. "He said he was going to find Kadin and give her purse back, but we all know that didn't happen. Regardless, you all made a better show of it than Vinnie, who didn't even put in an appearance."

"Great, can we talk about work now?" asked Kadin.

"No," said Olivan. "Not 'til you fess up about why you're avoiding Dahran."

"I decided to take your advice," said Kadin. "Dahran and I are finished."

Jace started and then stared at Kadin for long enough that heat rose to her face. *Does he know about Joelle and Dahran? Does he know that I know?*

"Hmm." Olivan frowned. "I guess it's good to avoid him for the time being, then. He's probably upset."

"Well, I haven't actually told him yet."

"Kay." Olivan moved to hop back up on the counter, but his disgusted face said he thought better of it. "You're supposed to break up with him and then avoid him. It doesn't work at all in the other order."

"I know." Kadin cringed at the whiny tone in her voice. "He was just... occupied last night. And then there was the murder. I haven't seen him yet this morning, and he's going to be so mad."

"Better just to do it," said Jace. "Like a Band-Aid and all that."

Kadin took a deep breath. "You're right. Of course, you're right. I'll talk to him later today, but in the meantime, can we please talk about the case?"

"Okay, yes. Now we can talk about the case," said Olivan. "Do you really think Mandrick Pane killed Philindra Dixie and Coelis Crest?"

Kadin shook her head. "I'm pretty sure he didn't. It wasn't his voice on the other end of the phone. But I didn't argue too much with Clout about it because custody is probably the safest place for Pane right now. By pretending she was talking to him, she put a great big target on his forehead."

"Besides," added Jace. "I'm not at all sure the same person killed both women. The modus operandi of the deaths was completely different. Philindra Dixie was shot in the head, with a gunshot loud enough that the body was instantly found. Coelis Crest had a heart attack, and Lady Beatrin only found her body by happenstance."

"Heart attack?" Olivan looked from Jace to Kadin, seeming to expect surprise from the latter. "So it wasn't murder?"

Kadin and Jace exchanged a long look. *Should we tell him?* Jace's eyes asked. *We have to trust someone,* Kadin tried to signal back. Jace looked away for a moment then gave her a slight nod.

"Is Dexter around?" Kadin asked. Dexter Gnome was Jace's fellow forensic analyst, the one whose mind the Society of Mages had allegedly destroyed twenty years ago.

"No, we're safe," said Jace.

Kadin turned to Olivan. "What do you know about Herrick Strand?"

Olivan spread out his arms. "Kay, it's me. What *don't* I know? He was Queen Callista's bodyguard, who was having an affair with her and killed her. He escaped custody and is still at large. I've got about five articles on his background upstairs in my office if you want more information."

"So you know what's common knowledge," said Kadin.

"Hey! My knowledge is not common! It is well researched and documented! I doubt you have five articles on the topic at your fingertips."

Actually, considering that Strand's escape had been her first and only real failure as a detective's aide and that she still considered him dangerous, Olivan should know her well enough to know that she had at least that many articles filed away in her desk drawer upstairs. But this wasn't time for a pissing match over who had a bigger stack of glossy articles.

"What I mean is that you don't know the truth about how he killed Queen Callista," said Kadin. "That he used magic."

Olivan laughed out loud. "Be serious, Kay. There's no such thing as magic."

"It's true," said Jace. "I examined the queen's body myself. Nothing natural could have caused the injuries she sustained."

"And I was there," said Kadin. "I was there when we tried to take him into custody. He used magic to burn everyone."

Olivan's face wrinkled up. He clearly wasn't buying the explanation. "If he's some kind of all-powerful murderer magician, why didn't he just kill everyone trying to bring him into custody?"

I stopped him. But Kadin wasn't ready to admit that, not out loud, and not to Jace and Olivan. "I don't know," she said instead. "I guess escaping was enough for him."

"Besides, I don't think he's all-powerful," said Jace. "I'm sure magic has limits, the same as everything else. But it does have the power to kill."

"So you think Herrick Strand killed Coelis Crest?" Olivan's tone was dubious.

"No." Jace shook his head. "I think magic of a different kind did."

"So you think there's more than one magic user running around Valeriel City, killing famous blondes?" asked Olivan. "Does that sound ridiculous to anyone else?"

"Sure." Jace shrugged. "It would sound crazy to me too, if I hadn't seen it in action."

"You can't tell anybody, Ollie," said Kadin. "And you can't do your thing where you give a million hints and let people guess. You have to keep this a complete secret."

"Oh, no issues there," said Olivan. "I don't want people thinking I'm as insane as I currently think you two are."

"Either way, if you take magic out of the equation, the different methods of death don't add up to one killer," said Kadin.

"But why would two different people kill two best friends in the course of a week?" asked Olivan. "And if it was the same person, what made him desperate enough to change his method?"

Kadin lifted her shoulders in a helpless shrug. Those were her questions too.

CHAPTER 12

WHEN KADIN GOT BACK TO the office, Fellows was waiting for her.

"Miss Stone," he said. "I received a most interesting call from CrimeSolve this morning. It seems that one of our homicide detectives—a man I had never heard of, strangely enough—attended a CrimeSolve investigation last night. I don't suppose you know anything about this?"

"Yes, sir." Kadin stood up straight. She doubted Fellows would accept her explanation, but she felt her actions the night before had been justified. "I interviewed Philindra Dixie the night of Coelis Crest's murder, before you told me to stay out of the case. I gave her my contact information and told her to get in touch if she had any further information to share. She called me last night, and I heard a ject shot fire while I was on the phone with her. I called our emergency services and asked them to investigate."

Fellows face turned red. "Let me see if I understand you correctly. Last night, you deliberately interfered in an investigation that I instructed you to stay out of."

"Not exactly." *I'm treading on thin ice.* "I have reason to believe Philindra Dixie's murder is unrelated, or at least only tangentially related, to Coelis Crest's."

"Yet the only reason you know about this second murder is that you were collecting information from Miss Dixie about the case you were explicitly forbidden to investigate." Fellows's voice rose with every word. "May I ask why you did not immediately refer her to me, the lead investigator on this case?"

Kadin swallowed. "Well, sir, she was very upset. It seemed rude to hang up on her. And of course, once I heard ject fire, I had to intervene."

"Miss Stone, there is no room for politeness in a murder investigation. Nor is there room for disregarding one's superiors."

"Yes, sir."

"You are excused for the day, Miss Stone," said Fellows. "Disobey me again, and we will see if we need to make the excusal permanent. Are we clear?"

Kadin squeezed her eyes shut. "Yes, sir."

Kadin headed for the autobus stop, her heels clack-clacking on the pavement in time with her beating heart. *I need to keep this job, especially if I'm going to break up with Dahran, which means I can't go find Baurus and get my purse back because he's going to ask about the case.* She was somewhat concerned about Xanidova, but if the revolver's behavior with Kadin was any evidence, Xanidova knew how to keep her silence.

I'll go home. It's Octavira's birthday, anyway. I'll give her some time off.

When Kadin got home, the house smelled even more delicious than usual. Most people's cooking put Kadin's to shame, but Octavira was in a class by herself. The scent of buttercream frosting permeated the air, and it was all Kadin could do not to seek out the source of the aroma and hopefully eat it.

As she turned the corner to the kitchen, Octavira

was putting the finishing touches on the frosting of an elaborate three-layer cake. Kadin's sister-in-law started when she heard someone in the doorway, leaving a line of pink frosting where it clearly didn't belong down the side of the cake.

"What are you doing here?" asked Octavira. "Don't you have big important detective things to be doing? Or is it your new joy in life to ruin other people's birthday cakes?"

Kadin cringed. "I'm really sorry about that. Can you fix it?"

"Of course I can fix it," said Octavira. "I'm not completely useless in the kitchen. I just shouldn't have to."

"I'm sorry," Kadin said again. "I got out of work early, and I thought you might want to have some time off today."

"Some time off?" Octavira snorted. "How do you expect me to have time off? Your brother went to all the trouble to get a roast for my birthday, which means I have to prepare it, along with my own birthday cake, as you see."

"Maybe I could help?" Kadin's offer sounded feeble to her own ears.

"You? Help in the kitchen?" Octavira shook her head. "Your brother went through a lot of effort to get this meal. We want it to be edible."

"Well, maybe you could teach me—"

"As if that's what I want to spend my birthday doing: giving you hopeless tips on a life you don't appreciate and are just throwing away."

She's clearly still mad about me breaking up with Dahran. "Okay. I just thought—"

"Go away, Kadin. Go play with the children or do whatever lofty, important things you do on your own time. No one wants you here."

Kadin steered clear of Octavira the rest of the day. She didn't have any lofty, important things to do or really anything to do at all. She decided to play with the children so she didn't spend the afternoon wondering if she even existed outside of work and her quest to find a husband.

By the time Tobin got home, Octavira had a veritable feast laid out for the family, consisting of perfectly pink roast, mashed potatoes, honeyed carrots, and homemade bread. Tobin heaped praises upon Octavira, and she gave him smiles of gratitude throughout the meal. Octavira even took her children's stories of the amusing things "Auntie Kay" had done that day in stride.

After the meal was complete and the children had devoured as much of the cake as Octavira would let them have, Kadin realized the time had arrived to give Octavira gifts. She found herself grinning as she went to retrieve the package from her room. For once, she felt she'd picked out something that her sister-in-law would like.

The children offered their gifts of hand-drawn pictures and plastic-beaded jewelry, which Octavira accepted as the most beautiful things she had ever seen. She doled an equal amount of praise on them as the chandelier earrings that Tobin presented her with. Then it was Kadin's turn.

Kadin handed over a rectangular package, and she ignored Octavira's sniff at the less-than-even wrapping job.

After Octavira opened the package, she gaped at the two books in her hands. "What are these?"

Uh-oh. She doesn't sound pleased. "They're biographies of famous surgeons. I thought—"

Octavira slammed the books down on the table. "Why would you think I would want something like that?"

"W-Well, I saw that you had checked that textbook out from the library—"

"Who gave you permission to go through my things?" Octavira's voice roared loud enough that the children cowered in wide-eyed fear. "Why would someone like me be interested in the lives of surgeons?"

Kadin had never heard her sister-in-law so upset. "I just... I thought..."

"Clearly, you didn't." Octavira spat her words. "Think, that is. I don't know why I put up with you in this house at all, Kadin Stone." By the time she was done speaking, tears had welled up in Octavira's eyes. She reached up and touched the wetness on her cheeks then turned and stormed out of the room and up the stairs.

For a moment, the rest of the family sat in stunned silence. Then Tobin cleared his throat. "I... um... I'll go talk to her. Kadin, can you...?"

"I'll clean up and put the children to bed," said Kadin.

"Thank you." Tobin breathed a sigh of relief. "I'm sorry, Kay. I don't know what came over her."

"It's fine." But it wasn't fine, and Kadin wasn't sure what she had done wrong or what she could possibly do to fix it.

CHAPTER 13

THE NEXT DAY, WHEN KADIN got to the office, she found a package on her desk. She checked the return address and recognized Philindra Dixie's apartment number. In all the scuffle over Philindra's death, she had forgotten the starlet had said she'd sent a package.

I should just hand it over to Fellows. And I will, just as soon as I find out what's inside. She picked it up and was surprised at the weight of the small package. Feeling around the edges led her to believe there was a book inside.

Because packages containing books have led to such great things in my life lately.

Kadin pulled the brown paper off and discovered a pink diary with embossed ballet shoes and swirly, foil lettering. Kadin opened to the cover page, where it read "The Diary of Coelis Crest" with a pair of dates that placed the diary around the time that Coelis left home.

This is it. This book has the evidence we need to figure out who killed Coelis Crest and, presumably, Philindra Dixie as well. She wanted nothing more in the world than to sit down and start reading the journal, but she knew she couldn't. Opening the package skirted the line already. She needed to go to Fellows and let him handle the evidence, or she would lose her job.

When Fellows got in—ten nerve-wracking minutes later than usual—Kadin stood up and, hands shaking, thrust the diary in his direction. "Philindra Dixie sent me this before she died. I didn't ask her to, and I didn't read it. I'm staying out of the case."

Fellows looked her up and down, as if trying to decide whether to be disappointed or pleased. He eyed the brown paper in the trash can. "You opened the package."

"It was addressed to me," she said. "I didn't read it. I'm staying out of the case."

"Very well, Miss Stone." Fellows took the book from her. "I have some urgent business to attend to for a new case. I'll have work for you tomorrow. For today, finish up the Mook and Tiara cases and have them to me by the end of the day."

"Yes, sir." Kadin wished she hadn't left only a few *T*s to cross on the two cases because she realized she was in for an incredibly boring morning.

I could go find Dahran and break up with him. It's probably better to do that in a public place like work. He can't get too angry here.

Her breathing shallow, she headed over to Dahran's office. She raised a shaking hand to his doorframe to get his attention before she realized he wasn't in there.

Oh. He's probably out on a case or avoiding me the way I was avoiding him.

Kadin went back to her office and watched her hands shake for about fifteen minutes before she had calmed down. *You're going to have to break up with him eventually,* she told herself. *You can't stay with him because you're scared of how he'll react.*

She spent the rest of the morning in a manner reminiscent of her first days on the job, back before Fellows let her do anything. She was about to leave for lunch when Olivan appeared in her doorway.

"Have you heard the news?" he asked. "CrimeSolve caught Coelis and Philindra's killer!"

Kadin froze, her coat in her hand inches above the rack. "What? They've publicized that they think it's Mandrick Pane? Did he confess?"

"Ugh, no, that's yesterday's news," said Olivan. "Come to lunch, and I will tell you everything."

I'm supposed to stay out of the case. But I suppose if Ollie knows anything, it must be almost *common knowledge by now.* "Okay. I was headed out for lunch anyhow."

Olivan refused to say anything until they were sitting in a relatively private booth in his current favorite restaurant, but as soon as they had their food, the floodgates opened. "So apparently Coelis Crest once had an abortion."

"Wait, what?" Of all the things Kadin expected Olivan to say, that was last on the list. In reality, it didn't even make the list. Society frowned on women having sex outside of marriage and taking birth control pills, but abortion was unheard of.

Olivan looked way too entertained for someone delivering such terrible news. "Apparently, when she was a teenager, her stepfather assaulted her, and she got pregnant and had to have an abortion."

"Ollie, that's terrible! The poor girl!"

Olivan's face fell. "You're right, of course. It's just so scandalous, and you know I love a good scandal."

Kadin gave Olivan a reproachful look, and he straightened up. "Right, empathy in check. Anyway, after Coelis died, Philindra was about the make the whole thing public, so the stepfather shot her to keep his secret. But CrimeSolve found the gun used to kill Philindra in his house, and it still had her blood on it."

Kadin took a bite of her salad, pondering. "How did CrimeSolve find out about all this?"

"Apparently, Coelis had a diary and shared it with

Philindra. Somehow, CrimeSolve got ahold of it, and it was sufficient evidence for an arrest."

"What?" *But Philindra sent the diary to me, and I gave it to Fellows. How did CrimeSolve get their hands on it? I guess... I guess there had to have been more than one diary? And Philindra sent it to both of us to make sure the evidence made it to light?* Somehow, that didn't ring true, but Kadin couldn't think of any other option.

"I said—"

"No, I heard you." Kadin sat back on the bench. "So Dove confessed to both murders?"

"Not yet," said Olivan. "He denied both at first but fessed up about Philindra's murder once they found the gun. It's only a matter of time until he caves about Coelis too."

Kadin took a bite of her salad and chewed, considering. "But what motive would he have for killing Coelis?"

"Uh, duh! He assaulted her!"

"No, I know. But Coelis wasn't about to make any of that public. It would ruin her career, if not her life. Abortion is extremely illegal, no matter the extenuating circumstances. Philindra was only going to make it public after her friend died because she thought it was relevant to the case."

"Exactly," said Olivan. "It was relevant to the case."

"I don't know, Ollie. Something seems fishy about the whole thing. Two totally different methods of death, two totally different motivations. It sounds like two killers to me."

"Oh, Deity, you're not back on the "M" word, are you? There is no such thing as—" Olivan glanced around to make sure no one could hear him. "*Magic.*"

"I've talked to a magic expert!" Kadin kept her voice low as well. "He seems to think the Society of Mages has their own motives for killing people."

Olivan rolled his eyes. "Kay, if magic existed, people

would have better uses for it than murder. Whatever kook you talked to was pulling your leg."

"He helped me catch Herrick Strand."

"And look how well that turned out. Can we please get back to the topic at hand? CrimeSolve found the scandalous killer, and you're just disappointed they got to him before you did."

"Maybe." *But I don't think so.*

Neither Fellows nor Dahran had returned to the office by the end of the day, and Kadin was mostly relieved. She didn't want to confront Fellows about how the journal she had given to Fellows that morning had ended up in CrimeSolve's hands, and she was terrified of breaking up with Dahran.

As she unchained her paper clips for the last time and put them away, her phone rang.

"Valeriel Investigations. Detective Fellows's office. Kadin Stone speaking."

"I thought I told you in no uncertain terms that you were supposed to solve that crime," came Baurus's voice from the other end of the line.

Kadin twisted the cord of her phone around her finger and thanked the Deity Baurus couldn't see her cringe. "I know. I tried. Really, I did. But Fellows wanted me to stay out of it, and CrimeSolve got to it before I could."

"It's fine," said Baurus. "Bay will never let me forget that the detectives she called in were the ones to solve the case, but it's fine."

"I'm really sorry—"

"Kay, it's fine, really. Murderer caught. Everyone is happy."

Somehow, the certainty in Baurus's voice made her feel like her fears about two murderers must be ridiculous. After all, if the duke was satisfied, who was she to gainsay him? "If you're not calling to yell at me, I can only assume you want to return my purse."

"I do indeed. Sorry I didn't get it back to you yesterday. The Assembly had a meeting about some nonsense, and I was tied up all day."

Kadin shook her head at the idea that the major governing body of Valeriel was engaged in nonsense, but she decided not to dwell on it. "No problem. Do you want me to come by and pick it up?" She hoped not. The Imperial district was short on autobus stops.

"Well, I was thinking that I didn't get the chance to properly appreciate the alleged best club in my city, what with you disappearing and all."

"I guess that's true, though I'm pretty sure my frequent visits are not what make it the best. And if I'm being completely honest, Ollie disagrees with my assessment."

"Your friend Ollie is insane."

Kadin didn't know whether to cringe or laugh as she imagined some of the things Olivan might have asked Baurus. "Again, I'm really sorry. Ollie is kind of an Imperial fanboy."

"I did pick up on that, thought I wouldn't use the 'kind of' qualifier." Kadin heard the smile in Baurus's voice. "What about you, Kadin Stone? Are you an Imperial fangirl?"

Kadin wasn't sure how to answer that. "Not really." She hated how her voice squeaked on the words.

"Fair enough. I'll see you at Divinity in an hour."

"Wait, I didn't say—" She heard a click on the other end of the line. "That I was going to go with you."

It's not a date, right? Dukes don't go on dates. They have arranged marriages and formal courting and stuff, right?

I'd better go see if Dahran's in one last time.

Dahran had not been in his office, and no one seemed to know where he was. She might have worried if playing hooky from work weren't exactly like him.

I should just go home, she thought as she stepped off the autobus at Divinity. *I don't need my purse that badly, and there are so many ways this could go wrong.* But she did need to get Xanidova back, and the truth was, she wanted to spend the evening with Baurus.

Stupid Ralvin DeValeriel. He had to get me thinking about things I want to do instead of things I'm supposed to do.

As much as Baurus infuriated her, she liked him. He was shameless, privileged, and any number of things that should have made her dislike him, but he challenged her, he listened to her—sometimes—and he made her feel like she was a real person instead of a woman whose only purpose was getting married and having babies.

Before she could decide that none of these, not even Xanidova, was a good enough reason for sticking around, a tall, broad figure made its way through the crowd toward her. "Kadin!"

She expected to get nothing more than a wan, queasy smile out of her face, but she found a broad grin stretching her lips. "You thought I wasn't coming."

"What? Of course you were coming." He held up a brown bag. "I have your purse." He leaned forward and whispered in her ear. "And your very interesting pearl-handled revolver."

Oh, Deity, did Xanidova talk to him? She decided to play it dumb for as long as she could. "You went through my bag?"

"Of course I went through your bag," said Baurus. "I'm only human, after all. And I'm only giving you a hard time about the ject. I know detectives carry guns, and it figures you'd have one as beautiful as you."

In her flustered state, Kadin focused on the fact that she

would have to carry around two purses for the remainder of the night. "Let me consolidate," she said, not meeting his eyes. "I can put one of these in the cloakroom."

After she had shuffled around her gear—and put Xanidova in the bag she intended to keep with her—Baurus held out his arm to her. "Shall we?"

Kadin moved to take his arm then stopped. She held up a finger. "This is not a date."

Baurus raised an eyebrow at her.

"I haven't broken up with Dahran yet, so it's not a date," Kadin repeated. "Baurus kept his face frozen in that same expression, so Kadin felt the need to keep rattling on. "I mean, not that it ever was supposed to be a date, but I wanted to be clear—"

"Kay, it's fine." Baurus's expression melted into a smile. "But you do have to dance with me at least once. Those are the non-date rules."

"I can handle that," she said with a relieved laugh. She took his still-proffered arm and went into the club with him.

An hour later, Kadin had to admit this was the best non-date she had ever been on. They'd arrived early enough that the club was still serving food, so they shared a flatbread. Kadin had expected Baurus to snub the simple fare, but instead, he told her stories about the time his mother had hired a cook who he swore was the worst Valeriel City had to offer.

"The man came so highly recommended from the Imbolcs, Mother decided she had to steal him," said Baurus. "But I think Delgata Imbolc was having one over on Mother in an attempt to get rid of this guy."

Kadin laughed, though she assured Baurus this cook could not be the worst chef in Valeriel. "I assure you, that is me. I mean, you've seen me try to make coffee, and everyone says that's ridiculously easy."

Baurus's other stories were surprisingly normal, considering his background. He told her about pranks he and Ralvin used to play on Beatrin.

"I wish you could have known him then," said Baurus, as if he were talking about some ordinary man and not the king of Valeriel. "He could tell the most appalling lies with a straight face. Since he became king, though, it's like the spark is gone. I can still see it in there sometimes, but I miss the real him, without the face paint."

Kadin reached out and lay a hand over Baurus's. She didn't know what to say about his pain at losing a cousin. The truth was, she probably knew Ralvin better than Baurus did at this point, and she couldn't say anything to make him understand that his cousin was okay.

Baurus flipped his hand over to hold Kadin's. "Hey, you owe me a dance."

Kadin had hoped he had forgotten about that, but she couldn't deny him, not when he looked so sad and lonely, and not when she felt so guilty about keeping secrets. "All right."

Baurus didn't let go of her hand as they headed to the dance floor, and she wasn't surprised when the music turned slow and soft as soon as they stepped onto the polished wood.

It's one dance.

Baurus pulled her close and wrapped his arms around her waist. She wasn't sure what she was supposed to be feeling as they swayed back and forth. She had never felt the kind of romantic surge she'd read about in romance novels, but this dance felt nice. She didn't feel queasy the way she did when she had to stand this close to Dahran. She enjoyed the feel of Baurus's rough cheek on hers and looked up in surprise when he pulled his face away.

He didn't look upset at her, though, and the rest of him stayed close to her.

"Kay, you're amazing."

He kissed her.

CHAPTER 14

UTTER SURPRISE SHOT THROUGH KADIN'S core. The duke of the entire city was kissing her in a very public place, even though she had been very clear this was not a date. She had no idea how to respond. Should she kiss him back? Rebuff his advances? Trinithy would know what to do. Olivan would probably have a flowchart for her next several actions, depending what she wanted the result to be.

That's the thing, though. I don't know what I want the outcome to be.

Those words. *"Kay, you're amazing."* She'd heard them before. Dahran had said the exact same thing to her the other night, and she knew she couldn't believe them from him. So how could she believe them from Baurus?

There's a connection between us, but I don't know him, not really.

The crowd's murmurs rose around her, giving her a very clear impression of how very public this ordeal was, and that made her decision. She did not want to be a public spectacle.

She pulled back, and Baurus—*Deity bless him for this if nothing else*—let her go. "What are you doing?"

He took a step closer, trying to bridge the gap between them again. "Kadin, I—"

She held up her hands. "No." She made herself look up at him, at the confusion in his darkened hazel eyes. "It's not... I don't... This isn't a date. I said that."

"You did, and I'm sorry. I just—"

Kadin could barely register his words. Had Baurus apologized to her? She couldn't look at him anymore. She couldn't look anywhere. She could feel the crowd's eyes on her. Her head felt dizzy, and she wasn't sure if she was confused or out of breath.

"I have to go." She turned and pushed her way past the people blocking the entrance to the club.

"Kadin!" Baurus called after her, but she didn't stop. She walked in as straight a line as she could out of the club and was relieved to see an autobus parked on the curb. She stepped onto it, not caring where it was headed, so long as it was away from Divinity and Baurus DeValeriel.

When Kadin got home, she hurried up to her bedroom, not wanting to face Octavira or Tobin after the last two nights' debacles. As she began her daily beauty regimen, she relaxed in the knowledge that she wouldn't have to deal with anyone until the next day.

"Excuse me," came a strident feminine voice from her bag. "Would you kindly remove me from this receptacle."

Crap, I forgot about Xanidova. Again. At least I held onto my bag while I danced.

She paused in the pinning of her hair and pulled Xanidova out and placed her on the nightstand by the window. "Are you speaking to me now, then?"

"Apparently," said Xanidova. "I demand to know why, when I was entrusted to your increasingly dubious care, you handed me over to a red potentiate."

Kadin stared at the ject, trying to figure out how the

weapon managed to communicate. Xanidova didn't have any kind of mouth so far as Kadin could see, yet she managed to be heard, loud and clear. Kadin shrugged and chalked it up to the elusive magic that seemed to keep intruding on her life.

"What's a red potentiate?"

Xanidova sniffed, once again a remarkable feat without a nose. "As if you don't know."

"Xanidova, I wouldn't have asked if I knew."

"You may have Gates fooled, but I can see right through you. I'm not giving you any more information."

"Fine." Kadin shook her head and returned to her seat in front of the mirror.

She had pinned about two more curls when Xanidova spoke. "Fine. A potentiate is someone with the potential to be a mage."

Kadin turned back toward the ject, not that she imagined it mattered. She couldn't read Xanidova's facial expression or anything. "Not everyone can become a mage?"

"No. Certain people—potentiates—have an affinity for one of the types of magic and, under the right circumstances, can learn to harness it."

Kadin thought back to her encounter with Herrick Strand, when she'd managed to stop him from hurting her. "Am I a potentiate?"

"You? Most assuredly not."

Kadin stifled a stab of disappointment that she didn't quite understand. She didn't want magic powers. "But Baurus is." *A red potentiate,* Xanidova had said. That meant Baurus had an affinity for destruction magic, like Herrick Strand.

He would want to know. Baurus wants magic more than anything in the world.

"I'd advise against telling him," said Xanidova, as if reading Kadin's thoughts. And who knew? Maybe she could. Kadin didn't know the rules of magic jects. "Magic does no one any good."

A thought occurred to Kadin. "Wait, you can tell whether someone has an affinity for magic by looking at them?"

"It's the first thing any mage learns," said Xanidova.

Kadin was surprised that Xanidova, who seemed to hate mages with a passion, had just admitted to being one, but she decided not to dwell on that. "Can you tell from a click?"

"No. I have to see them in person."

Kadin saw her own disappointed frown in the mirror. She had been hoping Xanidova could look at a click of Dove and determine whether or not he had blue magic. "Okay, another question. In your apparent expert opinion, would a mage kill someone with magic and then kill another person with a ject? And do a poor job of hiding the weapon?"

"Let me turn that into a question for you. Would you be that stupid?" Xanidova asked.

Kadin shook her head. She knew Xanidova was right. Kadin still had another killer to find. But how could she do so when she was forbidden from participating in what everyone thought was a closed case?

Kadin woke up Saturday morning with a queasy feeling in the pit of her stomach and couldn't quite remember why. Then the events of the last week rushed back to her—from Octavira's disastrous birthday to the murder she couldn't solve to Baurus's very public display of affection—and she wanted nothing more than to stay in bed.

No, I have to get up. Things won't be so bad if I face them.

She put on one of her more casual blue dresses and undid the clips she'd put in last night. Despite her resolution to continue on with her day, her thoughts raced. *What must Baurus think of me now? What do I even want him to think? And has Octavira forgiven me enough to let me help out around the house today? And what in the world am I supposed to do with Xanidova?*

The answer to that last one was easy enough. She would leave Xanidova shut in her room, where the children were unlikely to find her.

Kadin had barely made it downstairs when a knock sounded on the front door.

"Who could that be at this hour?" Tobin went to unlock and open the door.

Kadin peered around her brother and was surprised to see Ralvin DeValeriel, in his Vinnie Royal guise, standing at her front door, holding what looked like a newspaper.

"Good morning, Dr. Stone," said Ralvin. "I'm sorry to bother you at such an early hour, but I wondered if I might have a word with Kadin."

"And might I ask who you are?" asked Tobin. "I don't know how I feel about strange men visiting my sister first thing in the morning."

Deciding to head off the conversation before it got too awkward, Kadin moved over to stand next to her brother. "This is Vinnie Royal. He's Ollie's boyfriend."

Tobin's brow wrinkled. "The one who owns the newspaper? Why is he here before eight in the morning?"

"I don't know. Let me talk to him and find out."

Tobin didn't look convinced, but Ralvin appeared so bland and unassuming that Kadin thought it unlikely her brother would refuse.

"Okay, then," said Tobin. "But I'm watching you."

Kadin stepped out onto the front porch and shut the door behind her. "What is it?"

Ralvin gave a humorless laugh. "I came to ask how your night was."

"Interesting, terrifying, you know, the usual." Kadin's voice sounded hysterical to her own ears. Then she took in what Ralvin held. "Wait a minute. Why are you asking about my night? Did you talk to Baurus? Please, tell me you talked to Baurus."

As Kadin spoke, Ralvin slowly held up the newspaper in front of her. There, in bold lettering, were the words "Who Is Duke Baurus's New Mystery Woman?" Underneath them, in a picture splashed over half the page, was Baurus kissing her, and it looked for all the world like she was kissing him back.

Kadin's hands rose to cover her mouth, and her muffled voice emerged from behind them. "Oh, Deity. Oh, this is bad. This is so bad."

Ralvin lowered the newspaper and patted her on the shoulder. "Welcome to the Society pages. May it be your first and last experience with that particular toxin."

Kadin sank down to sit on the front step. "Don't you own the paper? Couldn't you have kept it out?"

Ralvin sat down next to her and rubbed her back. "First of all, I only own part of the paper, not the whole thing. And second, I have very little control over what actually goes into it. But let's look on the bright side. At least you broke up with Dahran before it happened."

"Oh, Deity." Kadin felt terrified tears spring to the corners of her eyes. "He's going to kill me."

Ralvin shot her a quizzical look. "Why? You, um, you did break up with him, right?"

"No." Kadin's voice was tiny. "I didn't get a chance."

Ralvin's face went slack. "What?"

"I haven't seen him! I got sent home early from work on Thursday, and he skipped yesterday!"

"Then why did you go out with Baurus?"

"He had my purse." The excuse seemed weak, even to Kadin's ears, but there was no way she could explain about Xanidova. "And I told him it wasn't a date. And I stopped him kissing me as soon as I could, but apparently, it wasn't soon enough."

"Well, on the bright side, you probably won't have to break up with Dahran now because I'm pretty sure he's going to break up with you."

"It's not funny! He might actually kill me. He has the worst temper."

"Yeah, he sounds like a winner. Real loss there." Ralvin sighed. "I'm sorry about Baurus. He forgets that not everyone lives in our bubble where every action becomes daily news."

Kadin sniffed and wiped the tears from her cheeks. "I don't think I'm cut out for that life."

"I'll talk to him," Ralvin said. "He'll leave you alone from now on."

Kadin nodded. "That's probably for the best." It didn't feel for the best, though. The idea of never seeing Baurus again filled Kadin with almost as much dread as seeing her face in the paper had. But odds were good he wouldn't want to see her after her performance last night, and she wasn't up for the kind of high-publicity life that apparently came with being involved with Baurus DeValeriel.

Ralvin drew in a breath through his teeth. "I really hate to leave you like this, but there's an emergency meeting of the Assembly this morning that Ralvin can't get out of."

Kadin decided to forgo mocking him for talking about himself in the third person. "Go. The nation's governance is more important than my petty concerns."

Ralvin gave her a sympathetic look. "It's not so bad, really, Kay. It'll blow over."

Kadin tried to laugh, but it came out as more of a snort as tears continued to pour down her face. Ralvin patted her back one last time then walked away.

Kadin sat on her front stoop, staring at the swirls in the concrete. A million emotions swam through her head, and she couldn't pick any one to concentrate on: embarrassment at her private life splashed all over the papers, fear at what Dahran and everyone else would think, regret that she was cutting short her blossoming relationship with Baurus.

She sat there for what could have been minutes or hours, spinning in her own head, until she heard a new set of footsteps approach her. She barely had time to look up and register Dahran's presence before he grabbed her by her hair and wrenched her to her feet.

"What is this?" The roar of his voice echoed through her aching skull as he thrust the photo of her and Baurus in her face.

The sharp pain on her scalp where he held her hair rendered her nearly unable to breathe. "I'm really sorry, Dahran. I—"

"Sorry?" Dahran shook her by the hair, causing ripples of pain along her scalp. "Not as sorry as you're going to be." He threw her against the stoop.

Kadin reached back to catch herself, and she heard a crack and a rush of pain down her arm as she landed on it. She thought about offering an explanation for her behavior, but she realized she only had one thing left to say to Dahran. "Get out of here, Dahran. We're done."

"You don't get to decide when we're done, bitch!" He raised his hand and brought it down hard on her face.

That's going to bruise, she thought, surprised at how calm her inner monologue was. She considered explaining that Baurus had kissed her, and she had extricated herself as quickly as she could. She thought about saying she had planned to break up with him anyway, if he had bothered to show up for work. But she knew that none of that mattered. The only thing that mattered was getting him out of her life.

"I do get to decide," she said. "We're done."

His face contorted with rage, and Kadin wondered how she had ever found him handsome. In his current state, his red face looked positively evil. It occurred to her that he might actually beat her to death, right here on the front stoop of her brother's house. She found herself surprisingly calm about the whole thing.

At least I stood up for myself.

As Dahran raised his hand to hit her again, Kadin heard the front door open behind her. "Step away from my sister, you miscreant," came Tobin's voice, followed by the all-too-familiar sound of a projectile weapon being cocked.

I didn't even know Tobin had a ject.

Dahran looked back and forth between Tobin and Kadin then spat at Kadin's feet. "This isn't over, bitch."

"Oh, yes it is—" began Tobin.

Kadin realized she couldn't let her brother do all the talking for her, so she continued. "Yes, it is. We're done, Dahran. Stay away from me."

Dahran threw the newspaper at Kadin's feet and stalked off. Tobin uncocked the ject—*Xanidova,* Kadin realized—and ran down next to Kadin. "Are you okay?"

Kadin shifted her position so her weight was no longer on the arm that had cracked. She looked at her palm and found the same concrete swirls she had been staring at as dents on her skin. "I think he broke my arm."

Tobin reached out and took hold of her wrist, which even Kadin could see was twisted at an odd angle and had swelled to twice its normal size.

"He definitely did," said Tobin. "Come on. Let's get you to the ER."

Kadin leaned over and gave her brother a one-armed hug. "You're not going to ask what all that was about?"

Tobin shook his head. "I don't need to. There's nothing you could have done that would warrant the beating that ass was giving you."

"And Xanidova—"

"Would that be the ject that shouted through the entire

house that I needed to go save you?" Tobin sighed. "Yeah, that, we probably need to talk about."

Kadin gave Tobin her first real smile of the morning. "I love you. But you're going to need to hear both stories. I'll tell you on the way to the hospital."

CHAPTER 15

KADIN SPENT MOST OF SATURDAY at the ER. Despite the odd angle of her arm, her emergency came in second place to the five burn victims from a fire on the other side of town. Fortunately or unfortunately, this gave her a lot of time to talk to Tobin.

He took the news about Baurus kissing her in stride. "I always knew you were born for greatness, Kay."

"I don't think having my picture blasted all over the paper for kissing a duke counts as greatness."

"No, but if you can catch the attention of nobility, you can do anything."

Kadin closed her eyes. "You need to stop saying things like that."

"I know Grandmother tried to drill your ordinariness into your head, but—"

"No, I mean..." Kadin shifted in her chair and cringed as pain shot up her arm from the motion. "I think it upsets Octavira."

Tobin fell silent, no doubt thinking of his wife's outburst two nights before. Eventually, he said, "Do you think Octavira is unhappy?"

Kadin looked her brother in the eyes. "I don't know.

If you'd asked me a week ago, I would have said she just hated me. But I think it's something more than that."

Tobin leaned back in his chair. "When I first met Octavira, she was a nurse at my practice. She was so smart and interested in medicine, and we had so much in common to talk about. She dreamed of being a surgeon, but she didn't have the money for med school. I fell in love with her and asked her to marry me, and for a while, we were happy. But slowly, she stopped wanting to talk about my job or the latest medical research. I thought she just wasn't interested anymore."

"I saw she had taken a surgery textbook out of the library," said Kadin. "That's why I got her the present I did. I thought—"

"I know. You didn't do anything wrong." Tobin sat back up and put his elbows on his knees. "I went to talk to her. I told her that if she still wanted to go to med school, we'd work it out, but she just yelled back that there was no point because she couldn't work, and besides, who would take care of the children? And of course, she's right. I think by marrying her, I ruined her life."

Kadin reached out and rubbed her brother's shoulder, an awkward task, since the arm next to him was the broken one. "You didn't. You said yourself she couldn't afford med school anyway, and it's not easy for a woman to have a man's career."

"Our society is so messed up," said Tobin. "Why can't women have children and husbands and jobs?"

"I don't know," said Kadin. "I don't know how to fix it."

"Me neither, but I guess I do need to figure out how to work on making things better for Octavira."

"Probably." Kadin took a deep breath and broached the one subject they'd been avoiding. "Speaking of Octavira, she didn't hear Xanidova yelling, did she?"

"I managed to convince her it was the neighbors," said

Tobin. "The last thing Octavira needs to know is that you brought a revolver into the house, much less a magic one."

Kadin couldn't help agreeing with that. "You don't seem surprised about the magic. Most people I talk to refuse to even believe it exists. But you knew it did, didn't you? How?"

"I didn't know," said Tobin. "Not for certain. But I've had my suspicions for a long time. And I know well enough to stay away from it, as you should."

"I tried to. Believe me, I did. But it keeps popping up in my investigations, and Daimon Gates says—"

"Daimon Gates?" Tobin's head whipped around to look at her. "You're not supposed to know Daimon Gates. Did he give you the revolver?"

"He's the only magic expert in the city." Kadin's voice was hot. "How do you know him?"

Tobin's eyes flashed. "He—"

"Miss Kadin Stone?"

Kadin was relieved for the receptionist's interruption. She couldn't recall a time her brother had looked as angry with her as he did at that moment. The nurse only wanted to take her vital signs and tell her she had to wait for a while longer, but they did give her some pain medication. When she returned to her brother's side, she was too woozy to continue the conversation. She found herself staring at the television in the corner of the waiting room, which showed coverage from the race Kadin had planned to attend with Dahran only a few days ago. Apparently "her" racer, the Yellow Comet, had won, though she couldn't see the appalling yellow color of his hair on the black-and-white screen.

When Kadin's turn finally came, she found the setting of her arm wasn't nearly as painful as she thought it would be, and after the cast on her arm dried, Tobin made a show of signing it in order to cheer her up.

The pain pills the ER doctors gave her knocked her out,

so it wasn't until Sunday that she had to deal with further fallout from her eventful weekend. Arm still throbbing, she listened to Octavira's lecture about how she needed to be more responsible. Kadin wasn't sure whether Octavira was more upset that Kadin's relationship with Dahran had exploded—thus keeping Kadin in the house until she found another man willing to marry her—or that the phone had been ringing off the hook all day Saturday. Either way, since Kadin knew from Tobin's words that Octavira's anger wasn't as sister-in-law-specific as Kadin had previously thought, she was able to take the angry words more in stride.

Kadin looked at the list of people to call back Octavira handed her and was surprised to see only two names on it: Olivan and Trinithy. Apparently, they had each called several times.

Kadin called Trinithy back first.

"How could you do that to Dahran?" Trinithy's voice was an accusing whine. "He's, like, absolutely perfect, and you cheated on him."

Kadin didn't know which false statement to address first. "I didn't exactly cheat on him. The paper exaggerated things—"

"Oh, I'm sorry, so that's not a picture of you and a duke kissing on the front of the Society pages?"

"And Dahran's not perfect. In fact, he—"

"For Deity's sake, Kadin!" Trinithy sounded so annoyed, Kadin would have thought she had personally offended her friend. "I'm not interested in another one of your ridiculous explanations about how a man is not good enough for you. You're too picky, and I hope you die single and alone!" With that, Trinithy hung up the phone.

"Ka-a-a-din!" Olivan sang with delight when Kadin finally got him on the phone. "Haven't you been a busy girl this weekend?"

Kadin sighed. "Are you going to yell at me too?"

"Are you kidding me? You kissed a duke. This is like my dream come true. Who's been yelling at you?"

"Oh, Octavira, Trinithy. Dahran showed up yesterday and broke my arm."

Olivan was silent for a moment. "He did what?"

"Well, I hadn't gotten around to breaking up with him yet, so it's understandable that he was upset—"

"Kay, that is no excuse for violence. Please tell me you are not blaming yourself."

"No, not exactly." Kadin cringed at how weak that sounded. "I mean, no. He was allowed to be upset. He was not allowed to hurt me."

"That's my girl." Kadin could hear the beam in Olivan's voice. "Now, on to important matters. Is Baurus DeValeriel a good kisser?"

Kadin slumped against the kitchen counter. "I don't even know. I ended it so fast. I was so taken aback, and I knew Dahran would be angry, and—"

"Hey, it's okay." Olivan surprised her with his understanding. "You're not used to having actual nice guys pay attention to you."

"Do you think Baurus is a nice guy?"

"I do. So what are you going to do if he tries to kiss you again?"

"I doubt that's going to happen. No guy likes being rejected." *Besides, Ralvin's going to tell him to stay away from me.*

"I dunno, Kay." Olivan drew out his words. "The guy seemed pretty into you in the click. You could be a duchess."

Kadin laughed out loud. "I doubt that's going to happen. I'm not exactly duchess material."

"Fine, suit yourself. Look, Kay, I gotta go."

"Sure thing. Plans with Vinnie?"

"Ugh, no. He's all busy. What do you think he's up to

all the times he's not around? Does owning the paper take that much time?"

He's off running the country, and yes, that takes a lot of time. "I dunno, Ollie. But you see him at least three times a week. Isn't that enough?"

"No, it's not." Olivan sighed. "I suppose that means I'm in love."

"Aw, you've been in love before. It'll be okay." In the four years she'd known him, Olivan had had any number of crushes and romances, though she had to admit that none of his previous relationships had lasted six months.

"It's different this time." There was a wistful pause. "Okay, I'll talk to you tomorrow."

"See you."

Kadin had some trepidation about heading into work the next day. She put concealer over the bruise on her face, though given the size and color of the mark, she could only do so much. And of course, she couldn't hide her broken arm.

People are going to ask what happened, and I can hardly tell them Dahran did it. He'll deny it, and people will say I'm trying to ruin him.

She found herself wandering down to the lab in search of a friendly face, not that she was sure Jace was a friendly face at this point. She wasn't sure of anything regarding her relationships after this weekend.

Jace was in the back room when she arrived, and he grunted a hello in response to her greeting. She saw him hovering over a microscope, and a body, presumably from the case Fellows planned to pull her in on this week, lay on the table.

"I'll be out in a minute," said Jace. "Make yourself at home."

Kadin leaned against the counter and tried very hard

not to look at the papers scattered everywhere. The dead didn't necessarily have a legal right to privacy, but Kadin felt she should respect it all the same. Nonetheless, one caught her eye—the blood test for birth control pills in Coelis Crest's blood. Aside from all the results being negative, it took her a minute to figure out what struck her about it.

"Jace? Is this a standard birth control testing form?"

The sound of running water came from the back room. "You mean Miss Crest's?"

"Yeah, why does it have seven test results in it?"

Jace appeared in the doorway, drying his hands. "Those are the standard tests. Used to be five, but they changed it about a year ago." His eyes came into focus as his gaze fell on her cheek and face. "Deity, what happened to you?"

Kadin shook her head. "It doesn't matter."

Jace came over to her and laid a gentle hand on her chin. He tilted her face up so he could get a better look at the bruise and hissed. "It was that asshole White, wasn't it? I certainly hope you're pressing charges."

Kadin looked into Jace's green eyes. She didn't think she had noticed the color before. She felt heat rise to her cheeks as she realized she was standing too close to him.

Kadin stepped back, and he let her go. "Yes, because that always goes well for women. It's fine. My arm will heal, and Dahran and I are finished. I'm more concerned about this." She thrust the paper in his face.

"Why are you concerned about that?"

"Because Isidri Tell told me he was providing faked birth control results to Coelis Crest. He even provided copies of the most recent ones, but they only had five tests on them."

Jace took the paper from her and shut it in a folder. "Well, you already knew he was lying. He must have performed Miss Crest's abortion. Taking money for falsifying birth control results is shady, but abortion is a serious crime."

"I guess," said Kadin. "It seems like a lot of effort to go through when the truth was she wasn't on any pills."

"You think there's something more insidious going on?" asked Jace.

"I'm a homicide detective's aide. It's my job to think there's something more insidious going on. I'm just thinking..."

Jace raised an eyebrow, waiting.

"Herrick Strand spent a year away from Queen Callista before he killed her. What if Isidri Tell hadn't seen Coelis Crest in as long? What if that's why the test slips were out of date?"

"That's a pretty big stretch, Kay."

"I know. I just... It feels right, you know?" She flashed him a smile, which hurt her bruised cheek more than she wanted to admit. "I'm going to go do some investigation on this. Talk to you later."

Before she could turn away, she found herself close enough to Jace to look into the green of his eyes again. "Be careful," he said.

"Of course." She said the words off-handedly, trying to ignore the intense look on his face.

Jace put his hand on her good arm. "I mean it. If Tell is a mage, you could be in a lot of danger. Bring backup."

"A lot of good backup will do against someone who can stop hearts," she whispered. "But I will."

Jace nodded and let her go. "Good luck."

Kadin returned to her desk, and when she saw Fellows was absent, she snuck back into his office. She had decided the best source of evidence would be the guest list for Baurus's gala. Fellows had confiscated her copy the week before, so she had to assume it was amongst his papers.

She didn't remember seeing Tell there, but there had been a whirlwind of people she didn't know. That a common doctor would attend was unlikely, but Kadin had to imagine the Society of Mages had their ways to finagle invitations. Or maybe he had been smuggled in with the help.

Kadin felt a pang of guilt as she cast her gaze upon Fellows's clutter-free desk, but she refused to let that stop her. She could not let Tell get away with murder.

She started with his top drawer. *Just envelopes. The list wasn't in an envelope.* She almost shut the drawer before the return address on the top one caught her eye. *Why is Fellows receiving mail from CrimeSolve?*

She knew it had nothing to do with the case, and she should leave it alone, but somehow, she found herself picking up the top envelope and pulling out its contents. Inside was a pay stub for a substantial amount of money. Feeling a chill run down her spine, she looked in the next envelope and the next. They were all the same.

I don't understand was her first thought, but even she knew she was being naive. These payments were why Fellows wanted her to stay off the case. This was how CrimeSolve got the diary. Fellows must have been on the take, collecting a paycheck from the bigger detective agency for letting them get credit for solving cases.

Barely knowing what she was doing, Kadin took one of the pay stubs. *I'll decide what to do about this later. For now, the guest list.*

She opened the file drawer and rifled through it until she found the not-so-surprisingly thin file for the Crest case. Inside was Kadin's copy of the guest list. She took it and hurried back to her office. She hid the CrimeSolve pay stub in her desk and pored over the guest list.

As she got further down the list, she worried she might have been mistaken. Isidri Tell wasn't among the guests or the serving staff. But then, five names from the bottom, under the vague header "Other admitted persons," she found his name.

I should bring this to my higher-ups before doing

anything. That was proper procedure, after all. Except her higher-up was Fellows, and he wasn't going to listen to her. She could go to Inspector Warring, but she hated to go above Fellows's head before she had a chance to decide what to do about his CrimeSolve pay stubs.

Besides, she did have the authority to arrest people on her own.

Backup. Kadin remembered her promise to Jace. *I need to bring backup.*

She called down to Personnel.

CHAPTER 16

"FELLOWS IS ON THE TAKE?" Olivan was, perhaps unsurprisingly, delighted at the piece of gossip. "What are you going to do about it?"

"I don't know, Ollie. If I tell anyone, it'll ruin his career. But I can't let it go on. Oh, turn here." They were approaching Dr. Tell's office.

"I mean, you could." Olivan turned onto Tell's street. "You're letting Dahran get away with beating you."

"That's different. That only hurts me."

"And who does Fellows collecting an extra paycheck hurt?" Olivan swerved into a curbside parking spot with ease.

Kadin unfastened her seatbelt. "Everyone who doesn't get their case solved because they don't have the best detectives on the case."

"The best detectives being you?" Olivan hopped out of the car, and Kadin followed suit.

"I don't know, Ollie. It's just wrong." She pointed at a window on the side of the brick building, where she had a good view of the doctor and suspected murderer sitting behind his desk. "Okay, you can see Tell's office through that window. Keep an eye on what's happening, and call for help if anything goes wrong." She reached into her handbag and pulled out Xanidova.

Olivan's eyes bugged. "Is that a ject? Since when do you carry a ject?"

"It's a magic ject." Kadin considered for a moment then handed the weapon to Olivan. "Xanidova, meet Ollie. He doesn't believe in magic."

"Well, isn't that just bully for him," said Xanidova.

Olivan fumbled the ject, nearly dropping her. "Unholy hellstones!"

"You're leaving me in the hands of this imbecile. Why?" asked Xanidova.

"Because I need to go in there and arrest someone," Kadin pointed to Tell's window.

"Would it be the blue mage behind the desk?" asked Xanidova. "I recommend just shooting him from here.

Olivan's face turned as white as Kadin imagined her own did. "He is a blue mage?" she asked.

"Of course," said Xanidova.

Kadin nodded. She had suspected as much, but knowing for sure made her all the more nervous. *How can I stop a mage? Maybe Xanidova's right. Maybe I should just shoot him from here.* She straightened her shoulders. *No, I have to give him a chance to surrender to custody. It's the right thing to do.*

"Ollie, keep an eye on anything going in there. If something looks fishy—"

"Shoot him," said Xanidova.

"Get help," finished Kadin. She gave her gun one last glower before entering the building. Olivan still seemed stunned. She would have to hope he came to his senses if she needed backup. She didn't want to wait outside the window all day, in case Tell saw them.

This time, the receptionist showed her right back.

"Miss Stone," Tell greeted her. "How may I help you? I

was under the impression Miss Crest's murder had been solved."

"New developments have arisen." Kadin breathed an internal sigh of relief that her voice did not waver. "You are wanted for questioning. I would appreciate it if you would come back with me to my office."

Tell leaned back in his chair and steepled his fingers. "I'm afraid I don't understand. If this is about the alleged abortion Miss Crest had, I can assure you, I did not perform it."

"No. This is about her murder, which you did 'perform.'"

Tell chuckled. "Miss Stone, the world knows that her abusive stepfather killed her. I wouldn't look too much harder than that were I you."

Kadin pressed on. "You lied about the birth control pills. And you were present at the scene of the crime. Besides, who better than a doctor to kill someone without leaving a trace?"

A maniacal laugh escaped Tell. "A doctor? Is that what you think I am?"

No, thought Kadin, but she didn't say it aloud. She didn't think the Society of Mages would be pleased if they suspected she knew any of their secrets.

"I don't need to touch someone to kill them," Tell continued. "As you are about to find out."

As a general rule, Kadin didn't pay attention to her own heartbeat. She didn't even think she was aware of its subtle presence in the background of her life.

She noticed when it stopped.

She clutched at the sudden pain in her chest and fell to the ground.

Tell closed in on her. "How does it feel to know you are powerless, Miss Stone?"

She tried to think back to how she had stopped Herrick Strand's attack. *I told it to* stop.

But how could she tell her own heart to stop stopping?

She couldn't.

She was powerless, exactly as he said.

She was aware only of the pain in her chest then a loud bang and the shattering of glass then nothing.

CHAPTER 17

KADIN AWOKE TO THE SENSATION of warm lips pressing against hers and a rusty scent filling the air. *Is it true love's kiss, saving my life?*

Her hazy mind could almost make out an image of whom her true love might be when she came to enough to realize she was coughing and lying on the floor.

"Oh, thank goodness, Miss Stone," said her rescuer, a woman with a matronly voice.

Definitely not my true love, then. She turned to gaze at Dr. Tell's receptionist through bleary eyes.

"I heard Dr. Tell say he killed Coelis Crest, and that he was going to kill you! I had no idea he was such a horrible man."

Kadin pushed herself to a seated position. "Ordinarily, I would say it's rude to eavesdrop," she said, her voice hoarse. "But in this case, I think I'm going to say, 'Thank you.' Where is Dr. Tell?"

Kadin followed the receptionist's gaze to where Dr. Tell lay in a pool of his own blood. *That explains the smell.*

"Someone shot him," said the receptionist. "He's dead. I don't understand—"

As if on cue, Olivan came running into the room. "Kay! Are you all right?"

"Now I am." She tried to rise to her feet, but apparently, being technically dead, even for a few minutes, took a lot out of her. "Thank you. If you hadn't shot him, I'd certainly be dead right now."

"Xanidova said—" Olivan cut off his words when Kadin shook her head and nodded to the receptionist. "Right, of course. I just—" He cut himself off as his gaze fell upon the puddle of blood on the floor and Tell's dead eyes. "Oh, Deity." Olivan looked sick. "Oh, Deity. I killed someone. I really actually killed someone."

"You had to," said Kadin. "He was killing me."

"I know. I know. I... He wasn't even touching you, but you fell. I had to do something." Olivan swallowed. "Was it really m—?"

"You saved my life." Kadin turned to the receptionist, interrupting Olivan before he could complete his thought. "What's your name?"

"Oh, I'm Bettany Lance," the receptionist said. "And I'm just happy I paid attention in those required resuscitation lessons!"

"I'm afraid it's not over," said Kadin. "We're going to need you to testify that Olivan shot Dr. Tell in defense of my life."

"Oh, that won't be a problem," said Bettany. "I'm always happy to do what's right."

On impulse, Kadin reached over and hugged Bettany. "Thank you."

The dust took a few days to settle, but with Kadin and Bettany's testimony, as well as some evidence from Jace regarding Kadin's health status, Tell's family decided against pressing charges. His sister even told Kadin Tell had always been a bit creepy, and she wasn't surprised by this chain of events.

On Tuesday morning, Kadin came in to find a dozen

white roses, already arranged in a lovely glass vase, sitting on her desk. She sighed as she picked up the card and was unsurprised to see Baurus's signature at the bottom. The note read "I'm sorry if I upset you. Ralvin says I shouldn't contact you, but I thought I'd give you a way to contact me." Underneath his signature was a telephone number.

Kadin didn't call. A large part of her wanted to, but her broken arm reminded her she was better off without both Dahran and Baurus for the time being.

During the next few days, Kadin looked back on her past cases with Fellows. In the six months she had been with him, they had shared jurisdiction with CrimeSolve on seven cases. In five of these, Fellows had specifically instructed her to work on other cases instead, and in all seven, CrimeSolve had been the one to collar the criminal. She didn't know how long Fellows's relationship with CrimeSolve had existed, but she knew she had to do something about it.

On Thursday morning, she took hesitant steps toward Fellows's office and knocked on the doorframe. "Sir, do you have a minute?"

"What is it, Miss Stone?"

"I know."

"You know what, Miss Stone?"

Kadin gulped. "I know that you take money from CrimeSolve to stay off cases where we're both called in."

Fellows glowered at her. "I don't know what you think you know—"

"I have evidence." Her voice grew stronger. "I haven't gone to Inspector Warring with it, but I will, unless..."

Kadin expected Fellows to deny it, to roar at her, to fire her. Instead, he sat there with a resigned expression, as if he had awaited this day. "Unless?"

"Unless you retire. You're old enough. You'll get a good pension from the company if you leave in good standing. I won't tell anyone, and you can leave with dignity. You can still do the right thing."

Fellows raised an eyebrow. "You realize you're putting your own career in jeopardy with your threats. There's no guarantee anyone else will take you on as an aide if I leave."

Kadin held up her head. "I know."

"Is that all, Miss Stone?"

"Yes, sir."

"Then you are dismissed." Fellows turned back to the papers on his desk.

Later that day, Olivan came in and plopped himself down on the chair in front of Kadin's desk. "I decided I've been wasting my life."

"Pardon?" Kadin had expected him to demand answers from her about Xanidova and magic, not announce he was moving to Ruathala or some such.

"All right, maybe not." Olivan gave her a smile that was still dimmer than usual. He pretended it didn't, but killing a man bothered him, even if he had done it to save a friend's life. "I mean, is there any nobler calling than reading up on Imperials?"

"Do you really want me to answer that?"

"Not really, no." Olivan took a deep breath. "The thing is, following you around on the case for the past couple of weeks felt like I was doing something with my life. I liked that feeling. I mean, I took that course on being a detective's aide mostly as a resume booster, but now I realize it qualifies me for a job."

"What job would that be?" *Please don't say mine.*

Olivan grinned. "You're looking at the new detective's aide for Robbery."

"Leslina's job?"

"Mine now!"

Kadin reached out to shake his hand. "Congrats, Ollie! Welcome to the club!" *For however much longer I'm in it.*

Olivan took her hand and gave it an exaggerated shake. "Now, you're coming clubbing, and celebratory drinks are on you!"

Friday morning when Kadin got into the office, a message that Inspector Blaik Warring wanted to see her sat on her desk.

This is it. I'm going to get fired.

"Stone," the ruddy-faced man said when she arrived at his office. "Sit."

She did so. "How can I help you, sir?"

Warring put his hands on his desk. "Fellows is retiring."

"Is he?"

Warring raised an eyebrow. "You didn't know anything about this?"

"I... may have heard rumors, sir."

"Hm." Warring eyed her but not in the lascivious way many men did. "I suspect there's a story there. I didn't think the old dog was going to retire for years yet. But I don't need to know the details."

"Yes, sir."

"This leaves me in a bit of a pickle. I need to hire a new detective. This new detective would definitely not get an aide immediately and would have to do a lot of work on her own."

"Yes, sir... Wait, on *her* own?"

"Do you want the job or not, Stone?"

"I mean, I... Yes, sir! Of course I want the job. I just—"

"Look, Stone. I didn't get this position by being an idiot. You solve crimes, and I need people on my team who can do that. The way I see it, even if you run off and marry your duke tomorrow, I've got one day of a competent detective I wouldn't have otherwise had."

"Thank you, sir!"

"You'll have to work with White." Warring's voice held a warning tone.

Internally, Kadin cringed, but she kept on a brave face. "I can handle that, sir."

"Well, then." Warring held out his hand. "Welcome to the team, Detective Stone."

www.ingramcontent.com/pod-product-compliance
Lightning Source LLC
Chambersburg PA
CBHW051922240626
47153CB00004B/1323